The Stonemason's Unwelcome Winter Bride

Cheryl Wright

Copyright

THE STONEMASON'S UNWELCOME WINTER BRIDE
(Unwelcome Brides Series – Book Ten)

Copyright ©2025 by Cheryl Wright

Small Town Romance Publications

Dedication

To Margaret Tanner, my very dear friend and fellow author, for her enduring encouragement and friendship.

To Alan, my husband of over fifty years, who has been a relentless supporter of my writing and dreams for many years.

To You, my wonderful readers, who encourage me to continue writing these stories. It is such a joy knowing so many of you enjoy reading my stories as much as I love writing them for you.

Table of Contents

Chapter One

Harrietville, Montana – 1880s

Laura Hartley pressed herself hard against the wall of the dark alleyway. She cringed at the way he'd dressed her – she was outfitted from head to toe in men's clothing.

She shuddered at the memory of her abduction. She was sitting quietly at her dressing table, brushing her long hair. Tears rolled down her cheeks, memories of the past days tugging at her heart.

She wiped them away then stared at her hazy reflection. Something moved behind her. She didn't hear anyone, but the mirror told her otherwise. From that moment, everything was a blur.

The calloused hand over her mouth, the cold, dark, eyes staring at her in the mirror, the smirk on his face, and the quiet voice warning her not to scream.

In an instant, her entire life changed.

It all happened with lightning speed, and there was nothing she could do to stop it. She'd been warned but didn't listen. Laura believed she was safe here in her childhood home.

Why he dressed her this way still baffled Laura. She was not precious, far from it, but she was not a ruffian. She glanced down at her clothes in the dark. No one would recognize her dressed this way. "Oh!" she squeaked, then slapped a hand to her mouth. She finally understood the disguise would make it easier to move Laura to wherever he pleased.

Her kidnapper didn't count on Laura's fight and tenacity. Her determination to get away. To rid herself of this evil man.

Laura slowly edged her way toward the main street. She couldn't stay in the alleyway forever, someone was bound to see her. The darkness had kept her safe so far, but for how much longer? Pulling the cowboy hat further down her head, Laura peeked around the corner. She could see a few townsfolk as they came out of the mercantile. The blinds were pulled down on windows, so she knew the mercantile was now closed. She could cross it off her list of possible hiding places.

The sheriff's office was much further down the street. She would never make it there without being spotted. Her eyes went from store to store, looking for somewhere to hide. Preferably not only for the night, but until Laura knew she was safe from her kidnapper.

Any other time, she would assume her father would have a ransom note by now. Not this time. Her eyes continued to search for a safe haven. It was then she saw the brightly lit building directly across from the alleyway.

She watched the sole occupant for a few minutes. Laura was unable to determine what he was doing, but he was concentrating hard on whatever it was. He suddenly glanced about, as though he felt her presence.

A shiver went down her spine. Laura had to decide now – stay put in the cold and dark alleyway, or hurry across the road and seek help.

Her breathing erratic, Laura rushed across the road, glancing about to ensure she wasn't seen. Running as fast as she could manage, she ran into the building where the mystery man worked.

Instead of asking for help, she ran right past him. His back to her, she hoped he didn't see or hear her. Except she couldn't ask for help that way. Laura hid behind a large piece of stone. Peeking over the top, she saw him. He was glancing about.

He knew she was here. Laura's heart thudded. He held a hammer in one hand, and a chisel in the other as he wandered about. Then he stopped. The next thing Laura knew, he was closing the door to his shop. She heard the click of the lock.

He had locked her inside. Her heart now felt like it would push right out of her chest. She was terrified when she was kidnapped, but this was a whole new level of terror. The kidnapper wanted her alive. This man seemed to want to harm her.

Why else would he carry two such dangerous tools?

Her breathing intensified the closer he got to where she hid, and Laura slapped a hand to her mouth, trying to keep her position secret.

"I know you're behind the stone block," he said sternly.

Laura tried to make herself smaller.

"I can still see you," he said. "Your absurdly tall hat has given you away." He seemed to chuckle then but didn't put down his tools.

Darn it. The hat was ridiculous, but the kidnapper swept her hair up under the hat to hide her gender.

"Put your hands up and come out slowly," he demanded. "I promise not to harm you."

Laura was torn. If she came out willingly, would he be true to his word? Or would the man attack? Especially believing she was male. "I'm coming," she said, her voice wavering. She stood, then lifted her hands in the air.

"Move out here where I can see you," he insisted.

Laura moved slowly and carefully. She didn't want to give the stranger a reason to harm her.

"Take off your hat," he said firmly. "So I can see your face."

She slowly reached up and held the brim of the large hat with her shaking hands. He watched her every move. How he would react when he saw her long hair, Laura was not sure.

No matter what happened next, she was in a power of trouble.

Chapter Two

Stanley Munro stared at the cowboy who had forced his way into Stan's workshop. He tried hiding, but that bizarre, oversized hat gave him away.

The cowboy stared at him, but hands shaking, he reached up to the brim of his hat. Stan couldn't complain, despite the slowness of his movements. His expressive eyes stared at Stan, his gaze never wavering. His hands held tight to the hat, and slowly lifted it off his head.

Stan's heart thudded. He stumbled backwards at the sight before him. A mass of blonde curls was let loose once the hat was removed. The trespassing young cowboy was not a cowboy at all. Nor was he young. Er, she.

Stan couldn't help but stare. He didn't expect there to be a woman underneath that disguise. His head was spinning. Why would a pretty woman such as this one, hide their face and their identity in this way?

"I'm sorry," she said quietly, then bolted for the door.

Stan dropped the tools he'd held.

His long arms allowed him to reach out and snag her before the woman could leave. "Oh no, you don't," he said harshly, then regretted his tone. There had to be a reason for her to dress this way. He dragged her over to the door with him and glanced outside to assure himself no one was there. Whoever was looking for her.

She kept her head low, as though trying to stop anyone on the street from recognizing her. Stan found it strange but knew he shouldn't. This trespasser was in grave danger. Perhaps not for her life. Not right at this moment, but one never knew for certain.

"Just let me leave, Mister," the woman demanded.

Stan almost laughed. She was petite and in no position to demand anything. As he held tight to her, she wriggled and squirmed under his grip.

"I'm doing you a favor," she said firmly. "If he finds me, he'll assume you helped me escape, and will kill us both."

Her statement stopped Stan in his tracks. His hands continued to hold her firmly, but now he lifted her and pulled the woman away from view of the street. This time taking her inside his cottage, out of the sight of anyone who happened to pass. Thank goodness the cottage was attached to his workshop, which meant they didn't have far to go.

He stared down into her face. The woman was beautiful, there was no doubt. But she was also pale, and her eyes glistened with unshed tears. She turned her head away, and Stan knew the reason – she didn't want him to see her cry.

He gently sat the woman down in his sitting room, nearest the fire as he could get her. It was freezing outside. She'd been out in the falling snow on one of the coldest nights they'd experienced for months. Her clothes were thin. Not made for the cold winter weather of Montana. She shivered as she sat, and her hands were shaking. Stan didn't know if that was due to the cold, or her situation. Perhaps it was a combination of both.

He reached for a blanket and laid it across her legs. Standing next to the fire, his eyes never leaving her, he stared at the stranger in his sitting room. Instead of bombarding her with questions, he kept quiet. Hoping she would open up of her own accord.

He didn't have to wait long.

"I'm truly sorry, Mister. Let me leave quietly, and no one will be any the wiser." She studied him, but Stan still said nothing. He could see she was getting frustrated with him, but this method worked. People usually disclosed their deepest secrets when he did this. "The kidnapper, he's after me, not you," she said, and his heart leapt. Kidnapper? She was a victim of kidnapping? His mind was reeling, and his heart pounding.

He decided it was now time to find out more. "Seems to me, there's more to your story than you're letting on," he drawled. "Let's start with your name." His words were demanding, and he expected a straight answer.

"Laura," she said, lifting her chin high in the air.

Stan pointed at her. "What's with the cowboy get-up?" He became more curious by the minute.

She closed her eyes and briefly shook her head. "My best guess? It was the kidnapper's way of getting me to his hideout without anyone recognizing me." She studied him again. "What's *your* name?" she asked gruffly, as though it had only now occurred to Laura, she didn't know who he was.

"Stanley Munro," he told her. "Everyone calls me Stan. I own this stonemason's workshop." He ran a hand through his dusty hair. "Why would anyone want to kidnap you?" he asked, keeping his eyes on her face. Not once had her expression changed since the moment she entered his shop. She held her face blank, as though ensuring he couldn't read her. It didn't bode well with Stan.

"I'm Laura Hartley," she said, keeping her blank expression intact.

His heart thudded. "Joseph Hartley's daughter? The textile tycoon?"

Her entire expression changed at his words. "Tycoon? My father was not a tycoon. He inherited his textile business, and the money that went with it." Her irritation at his words was clear.

"Family money. Same thing," he said gruffly. Stan had worked his entire adult life for everything he had. "I'm guessing you were whisked away by this low life, who intended to ransom you off to your father." Her annoyance was rubbing off on Stan. "Wait, did you say *was*?" He squinted at her, not sure what was going on.

The tears pooling in her eyes now freely flowed. "My father died last week. We kept it quiet to give me time to adjust to taking over his business."

Stan's head shot up. "Who knows your father died?" he asked gently. She was already distraught – her tears were proof of it.

"Only father's assistant." She swiped at the tears as they made a path down her cheeks. "The undertaker knew as well, of course."

"And his assistant, and the doctor who supplied the death certificate, the graveyard workers, and probably the entire town by now," he said firmly. "Someone knows you are the sole heir to your father's fortune. That's why you were kidnapped.

Not for your father's money, not directly. They want to marry you and have control of his empire."

Her expression barely changed. In other words, she knew exactly why she was in this situation. "Why didn't you have security?" he ground out. Having guards would have kept her safe.

She was angry at his words. Maybe now he would get some real answers. "Because no one was supposed to know about father's death." She swallowed on the words and swiped at her eyes again. "I was certain I was safe. At least for a while. Our family lawyer was working on the will and the paperwork. Once it was done, I would not have to worry."

"Your family lawyer? Which adds another person to the mix. The circle is widening," he said as he ran a hand across his chin.

She stared at him curiously. "You don't sound like a stonemason," she said quietly. "More like a…"

He interrupted her. "I am a stonemason and have been for some time." That could mean anything, and hopefully it stopped her from asking unwanted questions.

"Hmmm."

He could see the curiosity on her face, but didn't want to continue along these lines. Time to change the subject. "You must be hungry. I'll get you something to eat and drink. Stay put." The last words were a demand, not a question, and she knew it, he was certain.

Stan left her alone in the sitting room next to the fire, and hoped she didn't decide to bolt.

Chapter Three

Laura glanced about. The sitting room was cozy, and perfect for a small family. Apart from the adjoining kitchen, three, no, four rooms went off this one. She assumed they were three bedrooms and a bathroom.

Stanley Munro was a strange man. As much as he tried to put her off, he sounded more like a lawman than a stonemason. It made her wonder why.

If that were true, she thought he would take her straight to the sheriff's office and dump her in his lap. He probably thought it was the sheriff's job, not Stan's. And he would be right.

Except Laura didn't want to leave here. It was a perfect hiding place, and Stan seemed like a decent man. He didn't appear to be the type to hand her over to the local law and let her take her chances.

Quite the contrary. He came across as a man who had seen terrible things. And put them right. He was a big man – criminals would instinctively be afraid of him. Of that, Laura was certain.

Stan wasn't the kind to cross. Not that she really knew him, but it was the impression she got during the short time they'd spent together.

"Come and eat," he drawled, standing in the doorway to the kitchen, which was directly off the sitting room. "It's warm in here too. Bring the blanket if you want."

He turned his back on her then, and Laura heard him rattling about in the cupboard. By the time she sat down, he was pulling two mugs down onto the countertop. "Tea or coffee?" he asked, glancing over his shoulder at her.

"Tea," Laura said. "Thanks," she added. Despite her grief, and her dire situation, Laura was annoyed with herself. Good manners should never be forgotten.

"Eat the soup," he said. "It's good. I'll slice some bread for you."

She glanced up at him. For someone who was furious at her a short time ago, he seemed to have changed his entire attitude. His whole demeanor had gone from absolute anger to empathy.

Why was that?

Laura leaned in. She breathed in the pleasant aroma of the thick vegetable soup. "It smells good," she said. "Did you make it?" she asked, not expecting it to be the case.

He frowned. "I did, as a matter of fact. Is there a law that says men can't cook?"

Stan's answer shocked her. Few men knew how to cook, let alone make good, wholesome food. "Of course not," she snapped, then regretted not only her words, but her attitude toward the man who saved her.

Stan studied her. Trying to ignore his scrutiny of her, Laura kept her head down and took a mouthful of the delicious soup. She reached for a slice of bread, then buttered it. Not once did she lift her eyes to look at him.

Until the urge to do so overtook her.

His eyes had not left her face the entire time she'd sat in his small kitchen. They still watched her. Laura found it unnerving. He opened his mouth to speak, but didn't say a word. Instead, he turned away, then poured the boiling water into first a small teapot, and then into the mug waiting to be filled with coffee.

He placed the teapot on the table, but still didn't speak. Instead, he filled a bowl of soup for himself, and taking his coffee, sat down opposite her at the table. He continued to study Laura, and she continued to find it distracting.

Was he trying to work her out? Whether she'd told him the truth or was making it all up? If he asked, she would reassure him every word she said was true. She still wore the clothes she'd been wearing when she ran into his workshop. There was no choice but to do so. At least now she wasn't chilled to the bone. The warmth of Stan's home was reassuring. Along with the man himself.

Although she had to admit that Texas drawl of his was off-putting. Mostly because she wasn't used to it. Laura had lived all her life in Helena. Father's office was there, and the first *Hartley Textiles* factory had been built there.

According to her father, the business was everything. It was far more important than anything else, and that included family. When her mother died shortly after Laura's birth, he spent even more time working. A governess was secured to raise Laura. There was no choice. He couldn't stay home and let the business his grandfather had created fall part.

Laura barely saw her father in her younger years. Until she was older and he insisted she learn the family business.

The scraping of a chair brought her back to the present. An arm went around her, and that annoying Texas drawl whispered in her ear. "It will be alright."

A sob left her, and it was then Laura realized she was crying. Not for herself, but for her father. It hadn't even been two weeks since father had passed. She was kidnapped before she had time to properly grieve. There'd been so much to do, to keep the business running smoothly. Father would have insisted on it, she was certain.

Keeping his death a secret was the hardest thing of all.

She had relied on Drake to keep the cogs turning. "Drake," she whispered, and looked up at Stan with tears still swimming in her eyes.

"Drake?"

Laura wiped at her cheeks. "Drake Simmons. My father's assistant. He managed everything, an ensured the business ran smoothly after father's death. Made sure it was kept secret."

She saw the shocked expression on Stan's face. Shock turned to suspicion, then he went back to having that blank look he did so well. "How well do you know this assistant? This Drake Simmons?" His words were carefully chosen. She had no doubt about it.

It was Laura's turn to study Stan. "He…he's been with the firm for many years. Decades. He knows everything there is to know about it. Drake took the pressure off my father more times that I can recall."

Stan frowned. "Everything?"

Laura wasn't sure how to answer. "What are you getting at? Drake is a good man."

"As your father's assistant, he would have witnessed all the important documents, right?"

"Right," Laura said slowly.

"How long since your father updated his will?" His slow drawl and suspicious tone put Laura on edge.

She thought for a moment. "It wasn't long ago. When Father found out his heart was failing, he had his lawyer stop by." Stan handed her a napkin to wipe her eyes.

He didn't say another word. He didn't need to – Stan convinced her Drake was behind her kidnapping simply by the expression on his face.

Chapter Four

Laura stared at him with those big blue eyes. Tears pooled in them, but more than that, disbelief crowded her face. "Drake wouldn't…" Her words trailed off, and Stan knew she hadn't given it a thought until he brought it up. "He's a loyal worker, and a good friend to my family."

Or he wanted you both to think that way.

Already convinced, Stan kept his thoughts to himself. "You didn't recognize the voice of your kidnapper?" He had to ask. Laura was still grieving, which meant it would be easy to overlook the obvious.

"He…" She shook her head, then again stared at him with soulful eyes. "The voice was strange. It didn't sound…normal."

Stan's head shot up. "Not normal how?" He hated the fact he was interrogating this terrified woman, but it was the only way to help her.

Glancing down at her tea, Laura's eyes then went back to Stan. She reached out and took a mouthful of the hot beverage, clearly savoring the taste. "In the way we did as children. Pretending we were someone else." She studied him then. Her eyes suddenly opened wide. It was as though understanding had dawned.

"Drink your tea, and finish your meal," Stan said. "Enough talking for now." He stood, stretching himself as he did so. In the back of his mind, Stan was thinking. Seriously contemplating the information he now had at his disposal.

What he must do now was decide how he was going to save his house guest from the clutches of Drake Simmons.

~*~

With Laura settled back into the comfortable chair nearest the fire, Stan returned to the kitchen. She'd insisted on helping clean the dishes from supper, and he'd let her. Not because he thought it was women's work. Far from it. He could see keeping busy was what she needed.

Except once the kitchen was back to its former glory, they retreated to the much warmer sitting room. She had the blanket wrapped around her, closed her eyes, and leaned her head back. He wasn't certain if she was asleep, or simply resting her eyes.

He let himself relax into the chair opposite, his mind still churning with possibilities. It was then he heard pounding on the door. And yelling.

Glancing across at Laura, he decided she was asleep as she didn't flinch or move. Stan left the room to check the door. After all, kidnappers were not going to knock. More likely they would break down the door or shoot off the lock.

He glanced back over his shoulder as he left the sitting room. She was sound asleep. Stan hurried to the door. He could see the sheriff through the window, and the man's voice came through loud and clear.

As he thought, no kidnappers at his door.

Opening the door slowly, Stan ushered the sheriff inside. "Everything alright here?" he asked Stan, curiosity written all over his face.

"Why do you ask?" Stan replied as he scanned the street for possible kidnappers. Stan closed and locked the door behind him.

Colt watched as Stan did the very things he never did. "You never close the door. Nor do you lock it. You've done both." Sheriff Colt Turner stared at him. "Should I be worried?"

"Would you like a coffee, Sheriff?" Stan was already walking toward the kitchen and assumed Colt would follow.

"You never call me Sheriff. What's up?"

He gestured for his visitor to sit at the table, then poured them both a mug of coffee. Once they had both fortified themselves for what was to come, Stan told him the story of his unexpected guest.

"Well, dang," Colt said. "This is not what I expected to hear. I was concerned you'd had an accident of some sort." The sheriff frowned. "You want me to take the little lady off your hands?"

Stan didn't hesitate. "Not at all. We've connected. She's talking to me, and I see it as a positive."

The sheriff nodded. "Well, you have the skills to get answers."

Stan shushed the man sitting opposite. "I haven't told her. Not yet."

"Told me what?" Laura said, her voice still full of drowsiness.

He first glared at Colt, then Stan turned to face Laura. "Only that you should stay here for the time being." Her face portrayed her disbelief in his words. It wasn't like he wasn't telling the truth. Not really. He'd already made the decision, long before Colt had arrived. "Laura, this is Sheriff Colt Turner. He came to check if everything was alright."

Laura stared at the two men. "Why?"

The simple word had him confused. Until he understood.

"Stan never closes the door during the day. Or locks the door." The sheriff's eyes wandered from Laura to Stan. They held more questions than answers.

Thankfully, Colt glanced down at the note in his hand. The list of tasks Stan had set for him. "I'll get this done – first thing tomorrow."

Stan's eyes ran over the message once more. *Getting married STOP need your expertise STOP*

Despite Colt's concern the message wouldn't be understood, Stan knew it would be. Assistance would be dispatched as a matter of urgency. "I have much to do, so I'll be on my way," he told them both. "You take care, Miss Hartley. Stay off the streets in case those kidnappers are still here."

"Kidnapper," she corrected. "I only saw one person. A man about your height. He had a quiet voice and soft hands."

"In other words," Colt said. "Not your average kidnapper."

Colt's words rang true. Most kidnappers were rough around the edges. They didn't have the patience and generally barked out orders. Stan couldn't recall ever hearing a victim describe their kidnapper as having a quiet voice.

"Soft hands?" Stan asked, thinking out loud. "Like someone who worked in an office all day?"

Laura turned to Stan. "Maybe you were right all along. Perhaps it was Drake, but I honestly don't think so." He put a hand to her shoulder. She might come across as holding it all together, but the way her body shook under his touch said something completely different.

Stan had given the sheriff some necessary tasks. They would hopefully provide more answers than questions. Colt held the note in his hands. "I'll get back to you when I have answers," he said quietly.

"What answers?" Laura demanded. Instead of answering, Colt tipped his hat and walked out of the kitchen. Stan followed behind, leaving Laura alone in the small room to contemplate her situation further.

Chapter Five

Laura wasn't sure what just happened. What was clear though, was the two men had concocted some sort of plan. They obviously didn't want her to know what that plan was. If she wasn't a woman being hunted and trying to keep a low profile, she might have protested.

And if she wasn't fast heading toward the wrong side of forty, she might have stomped her foot in protest. Except she'd never done such a thing. She had been brought up to behave as a lady should.

She was startled when Stan returned from locking the door behind the sheriff. "You and the sheriff are thick as thieves," she stated. There was no doubt in Laura's mind they were like peas in a pod. So much alike, especially when it came to planning things behind her back.

For a moment, she thought Stan wasn't going to answer. She studied him as he stood in front of the fireplace, leaning against the mantle. While she studied him, he studied her. It seemed like they were at a stalemate. "I suggested Colt get a copy of your father's will," he finally said.

Did he now realize she had a right to know what was going on? After all, this was her life at stake. Not that she'd been threatened with death. Not really. "Why would someone want to kidnap me?" She didn't mean to say the words out loud, but the words flowed out of her mouth unhindered.

Stan watched her closely. "Normally, for ransom. Except this time,"

She interrupted him. "This time," she continued, "there was no one left to receive and process a ransom." The circle of people who knew her father had died was small. Even with the undertaker, the graveyard staff, and others, as Stan had pointed out. They'd all been paid well to keep quiet. Drake knew everything there was to know about her father's business. "Drake would have witnessed Father's amended will."

"Which means he knows exactly what is in it." Stan stepped toward her. "Do you?" he asked, sitting down opposite her, close to the edge of his chair.

Shaking her head, Laura's heart pounded. Her father would be heartbroken if he were here now. He'd believed Drake to be a loyal employee. More than that, he'd considered Drake a friend.

Except a friend would not capture his daughter and hold her captive. Laura couldn't believe what was happening. She shook her head again, trying to shake her negative thoughts away. "Father and I discussed Drake. He suggested an appropriate amount was given to Drake as a way of showing his appreciation."

"Except Drake didn't know?"

"Not at all." In hindsight, he should have been told. It would have avoided all this…unpleasantness.

Stan sat further back in the chair. He scratched his head. "Why didn't he tell Drake? Or have it listed in his will?" He thought for a moment. "Did your father worry Drake might harm him?"

Laura felt shocked at the suggestion. "Why would you ask such a thing?" Her voice was wavering, and she felt light-headed. "Do you think Drake murdered my father?" She swallowed back the emotion that threatened to overtake her once more.

"That's not what I was suggesting. It appears Drake was aware of your father's illness, so no need to eliminate him."

Laura breathed a sigh of relief. "I don't see Drake as a killer," she said quietly. "And I also don't believe he is capable of kidnap."

Stan reached out and held her hands. His large hands dwarfed hers. They gave her comfort, but she also felt safe with Stan. It was as though nothing would harm her with him around. Laura shook herself mentally. She'd known this man for only a matter of hours, and she was putting her life in his hands?

Except, there was something about him. He spoke as though he knew how a criminal's mind worked. Like he had personal experience with them. It had her wondering about his past. Stan might tell her he was a stonemason, and clearly, he was.

Her instincts told her there was far more to Stanley Munro than he was willing to share.

~*~

Laura spent the rest of the evening in the sitting room, lapping up the warmth of the fire. Stan sat opposite her, but neither spoke.

There was a companionable silence, with neither needing to speak or to ask questions. Until she began to doze.

"It's late," Stan said quietly. "We should retire for the night."

Her heart pounded. "Is it safe? Should we force ourselves to stay awake…just in case?" A slight smile touched his lips, but Laura knew he wasn't laughing at her. He was merely imagining her trying to force herself awake for the night. She had barely stayed awake for the past hour.

"It's safe," he said, the brief smile completely gone. He reached out and helped Laura to her feet. "You looked utterly exhausted." She felt that way, too. Stan led her to the main bedroom – it wasn't where she expected to be taken.

Confusion overtook her. Surely, she could sleep in one of the spare rooms? "I can't sleep in here, with you," she said firmly. "It wouldn't be right."

That fleeting smile reappeared and left as quickly as it had arrived. "It's for your own safety. I don't expect anyone to break in, but if they do, I can't protect you if you're in another room."

It made perfect sense. Still, the thought of sleeping in the same bed as a complete stranger…

"I won't touch you, I promise," he said. Laura had no choice but to believe him. Stan went to a chest of drawers sitting in the corner of the room and pulled out a nightshirt. "You can wear this to bed. It will be too big, but better than nothing."

Laura was shocked at his words but knew it to be the truth. Without borrowing one of his shirts, she had nothing but her undergarments. The sooner she got this horrible cowboy outfit off, the better. She was far too stressed to even think about it earlier.

"I'll leave you alone to change," Stan said, little clouds of pink staining his cheeks. Was he embarrassed? She couldn't imagine a man of his age feeling that way, but she knew nothing about him. It meant anything was possible.

The moment the door closed behind her, Laura shed those awful clothes she was forced to wear, and put on the oversized shirt. She neatly folded the discarded clothing and placed them on a chair. Why, she didn't know, but felt it was the right thing to do. She climbed into bed, pulling the covers up around herself, then drifted off to sleep.

Chapter Six

Stan pottered about while Laura prepared for bed. He couldn't, in all consciousness, let her sleep alone in the spare room. If anything happened to her, he would carry the guilt for the rest of his life.

He had a plan, and first thing tomorrow morning, Sheriff Turner would put it into action. Thankfully, Colt was willing to go along with him and would ensure his message was sent. The last thing either man wanted was for a kidnapper to put fear in the townsfolk of Harrietville.

Despite Laura believing Drake wouldn't harm her, and didn't murder her father, Stan knew better. Once people like Drake Simmons decide they want someone else's wealth, they usually didn't give up. He was convinced this situation was no different. He could feel it in his gut.

He added more logs to the fire in the sitting room, and also to the kitchen stove. He filled the kettle ready for the morning, then did a walk around. Stan ensured every door was bolted, every window was closed, and there was no way of entry for anyone who thought about reaching Laura.

He felt certain her father's assistant didn't plan on killing her. Not yet, anyway. Stan knew his type – Drake would force her into marriage, so he had control of her father's estate. After what Drake deemed an acceptable amount of time, Laura would meet with a terrible accident.

There was only one cure for men like that, and the solution was jail for life. If Colt was able to get hold of the will, or at least find out the contents of it, Stan would know what he was dealing with.

If the lawyer was unwilling to disclose the information, it would slow everything down. It wouldn't be a good thing, since he wanted to get everything sorted sooner rather than later. For Laura's sake.

He yawned. Stan knew he wouldn't be any good to Laura if he was sleep deprived. He did another check of all the doors and windows, and finally satisfied, he went back to the house and bolted the door there.

It hurt his heart to even contemplate it, but he went into the second spare room, which he used as an office. There he removed the piece of art from the wall, and carefully unlocked the safe. He momentarily stared at the pistol sitting in the holster and removed it. The packet of bullets was taken from the safe as well. Stan hoped he didn't need to use the gun, but better safe than sorry. He would not take a chance on Laura's life. Or anyone else's.

Tomorrow was sure to be busy. He needed to get proper clothes for Laura and talk to the preacher. There were a couple of orders to be done, including a fireplace surround, but they weren't urgent. He would get to them when it was safe. Or possible.

He carefully and quietly opened the bedroom door. Laura was sound asleep. It wasn't like he was surprised – at one point, Stan was convinced he'd be carrying the sleeping woman to bed. It would be no burden at all. She was such a petite creature; he was certain she would be a light-weight.

Under the cover of darkness, Stan began to remove his clothing, then reconsidered. Fully dressed was a more sensible option. If there was an intrusion through the night, he wanted to be prepared. It was unlikely, but Stan needed to be ready for anything.

Drake Simmons was a desperate man. Who knew what he would do to get his hands on Joseph Hartley's fortune?

Or his daughter?

The mere thought of it sent shivers down his spine.

Tomorrow would ensure Drake could no longer force marriage on Laura, but that didn't mean he wouldn't still try to harm her. Stan hadn't discussed his plan with his unexpected guest, but that was a conversation for another time.

He knew what would deter the man, and was certain Laura would go along with his plans.

At least he hoped she would.

Removing his boots and pushing them aside, he climbed in under the covers with Laura. She slept soundly, not so much as flinching when he entered the bed. He slipped his gun under the pillow, having loaded it before entering the bedroom.

Stan knew he couldn't assume anything and couldn't take chances. Laura's life depended on it.

~*~

Early signs of dawn were creeping through the window when Stan awoke. Laura was sitting on the edge of the bed. "Good morning," he whispered, trying not to startle her.

She spun around to face him. "Good morning," she replied. "Did you sleep well?" she asked, gazing over his fully clothed body, but not mentioning it.

"I did," he told her, knowing it was a complete lie. He lay awake most of the night, listening for unusual sounds. Thankfully there were none. Stan rolled over and slid out of bed. Laura turned away and stood. She seemed a little weak on her feet.

She had been unable to tell him how long ago she'd been kidnapped, or how many days Drake had held Laura against her will. What was clear to him was Drake had drugged her. Otherwise her mind wouldn't be so confused.

He would never completely understand the way criminals thought. Drake was going to be looked after in Joseph Hartley's will, even if it wasn't stated on paper. More likely than not, Laura would have kept him on as her assistant. Her father had no issue with Drake, so it was unlikely Laura would.

Instead, Drake became impatient and couldn't control his temper. He lashed out at the one person who was already arranging a large bequest for him. In Stan's mind, there was no one else who would benefit from Laura's abduction. And for no other reason than to force her to marry him.

Drake was a fool. There was no other way to put it. Once the lawyer finished the paperwork, his inheritance would have been secured.

Stan shook his head.

Money. It was always the downfall of even the greatest men. In this instance, Drake Simmons not only lost out on the bequest, but would live much of his life in jail.

Reaching under the pillow, Stan pulled out the gun and tucked it into his waistband. Laura gasped.

"We don't know what we're dealing with," Stan told her. "I promise not to use it unless absolutely necessary." He couldn't guarantee anything more.

41

Chapter Seven

Laura stood at the edge of the bed while she got her bearings. She felt incredibly weak. Until recently, Drake had always treated her kindly. Since her father's death, or should that be, since he kidnapped her, all that changed. She couldn't recall him giving her food at any point. Nor did he provide tea or water.

Still, her mind was fuzzy. Whatever he'd used when he snatched her still lingered.

Stan came around to her and took Laura's hands. "I'm fine," she said quietly, knowing it was a complete lie. Her pride got in the way of accepting this man's help. He had been nothing but kind, and she repaid him with blatant untruths.

He stared down into her face. "I beg to differ," he said gently. "You are unstable on your feet." Without further comment, Stan lifted her and carried Laura into the sitting room. She didn't complain, instead enjoyed having his arms around her. The comfort she'd felt with him yesterday was tenfold today.

She'd never really bothered about men. Laura was too busy with her various charities and helping out in the business where she could. Father had been slowly teaching her how to take over. They both knew his death was inevitable.

Stan carefully placed her on the chair next to the fire and covered her with a blanket. "I need to make breakfast," she growled. Stan took no notice.

"Stay here," he demanded. "I am very capable of cooking." He disappeared out of the room before she could protest further. Laura basked in the warmth of the fire. Stan's home was warm and cozy. It felt more like home than her own home.

The family home was a sprawling mansion, and with only two of them living there, she'd begged her father to downsize. Even the stables were huge. Built when her grandfather was the owner, it was built to house not only his family, but several servants.

Laura saw it as an absolute waste for two people and had visions of it making a wonderful refuge for the homeless. Or an orphanage. Father would have none of it. To Joseph Hartley, appearances were everything. She barely remembered her grandfather, but from what she'd been told, he was of the same opinion. *The rich must portray their superiority*, he would say whenever the opportunity arose.

Her father often quoted those same words. It churned Laura's stomach to think her own family did not have the compassion required to help those in need.

"Here you are. A hot mug of tea." Stan put the tea on the side table. "Breakfast won't be long," he said. "We can eat in here if you like?"

She glanced up into his face. Stan was a kind man. A decent man. He also had his secrets. She hadn't known him for long when she'd come to that conclusion. Every time he opened his mouth, his secrets spilled out alongside his words.

She knew more about Stanley Munro than he would likely ever tell her.

It had been a long morning of doing nothing but eat, drink, and lap up the warmth of the fire. The flames from the fire were mesmerizing, and Laura found herself dozing off on more than one occasion.

With lunch finished, Laura decided she needed to plan supper. She couldn't allow Stan to do everything. Especially when preparing meals and cooking was traditionally women's work.

Stan protested, but Laura chose to ignore him and rummaged in the pantry. She wasn't the best cook in the world, but she wasn't the worst either.

Despite her father's wealth, they had not employed a cook for many years. When she was younger, their young cook also looked after Laura. She was more like a governess than a family cook. With only Laura and her father, it seemed a relatively easy job, but Daisy had her hands full.

Memories of life with Daisy came flooding back, and Laura longed for those days to return. Daisy would hug her whenever it was needed, and Laura would be safe again. Except she knew it was impossible. Turning back the clock would give her back her parents.

An impossible feat, but one Laura longed for.

She reached for the vegetables she wanted and carried them into the kitchen. Stan sat at the table. That was the deal – if she did the cooking, which she'd demanded to do – he would stay close by.

He was a likeable man. Despite that Texan drawl of his.

The thought made her smile. She'd grown rather used to his accent. Truth be told, she'd grown used to the man. He was caring and protective. It was exactly what she needed right now. But what of his business?

Laura placed the vegetables on the countertop. "You need to work," she said firmly. "I'm fine here." Without waiting for a response, she hurried back into the pantry. The icebox was not huge, but she hoped there was some usable meat in there. If not, she would have to change her plans for supper.

Lifting the lid and finding what she'd hoped, Laura scanned the other items. Milk and butter. She would put those to the back of her mind for another time. Her eyes went to the pantry shelves. Flour and sugar. Basic ingredients that would come in useful.

Perhaps Stan wasn't joking when he told her he cooked for himself. Laura shrugged the thought away and headed back to the kitchen. "Is it alright if I use this beef?"

"It's there for the taking. Everything is."

He didn't say much, but his expression told Laura he was relishing whatever she was making. She only hoped it turned out the way it should.

Laura spent the next thirty minutes cutting and browning the meat, then chopping the vegetables ready for the stew. Ideally, she should have started straight after breakfast. Short of admitting it to Stan, she'd felt weak, so took the morning to recover her strength.

She was almost back to normal now and pottered about collecting everything she needed.

"Why don't you let me help?" Stan asked. "Instead of making several trips to the pantry and back."

Laura knew it made sense, but she wasn't sure what she'd needed, and it was easier this way. "I think I'm done now but thank you for the thought." She smiled at him, and Stan grinned.

"I should have told you earlier – we might have an extra mouth or two to feed tonight." He seemed rather somber, and Laura couldn't understand his sudden change of mood.

"Oh?" she asked, wondering who was expected.

Instead of answering, he gave her titbits of information. "The sheriff will be here later, along with the preacher."

Stan mentioned something about the preacher yesterday, didn't he? Except he hadn't given her any more information. Exactly what he was doing to her now.

"Why is that?" she asked. When he didn't answer, Laura continued. "I understand the sheriff, since you gave him several tasks, but not the preacher. This time she glared at him, silently telling Stan she expected an answer.

"It's like this," Stan said, his eyes not meeting hers. "The preacher is coming to marry us. No wait," he said, indicating with his hands for her to not interrupt him. "I believe Drake Simmons kidnapped you to get hold of the family fortune. If you are married, there is no reason or incentive for him to try and kidnap you again."

Laura stared at him and blinked. *Was he crazy? Marry him?* They barely knew each other beyond their names.

"It will be a marriage of convenience," he quickly added. "We can have it annulled when your kidnapper is captured and in jail."

"Of course. That would be the best option," Laura added. At this point, she would do almost anything to feel safe again. She only hoped Stan's plan worked.

Chapter Eight

The look on Laura's face told Stan all he needed to know. She was not thrilled to be marrying him.

It wasn't as though he was interested in her father's fortune. Although technically it was now her fortune. At least it would be the moment her family lawyer had all the paperwork sorted.

It bothered him that Drake had not identified himself to Laura. Had he done so, he was certain she would have told him about the large bequest her father wanted him to have. Surely Drake would have then backed off before it was too late.

Except he didn't. He carried through with the kidnapping. He drugged his employer's daughter and took her from her home.

If Drake Simmons truly saw himself as a friend to Joseph Hartley, why would he do such a thing? It was niggling at the back of Stan's mind. Clearly Simmons was not a criminal. Although, pushed to the edge, no one truly knew what a person would do to right what they deemed a wrong.

Pounding on the door startled Laura. He reassured Laura it was likely either the sheriff or the preacher. Or it could be a friend of Stan's. Either of those options worked for him, but not if it was anyone else.

With his holster around his waist holding his fully loaded gun, Stan headed toward the door. Through the glass pane, he could see the sheriff. Stan unlocked the door and let him pass. "I sent your message," he said, sounding breathless. "But haven't had a response."

Stan didn't expect one.

"I arranged the preacher, and my wife arranged clothes for Laura."

Stan thanked him, but his mind was elsewhere. "I've been thinking," he said as he locked the door again. "Perhaps the wedding should be at the church. Out in the open. We could arrange a reporter to be present. That way it will be in the newspaper and…" One look at the expression on the sheriff's face and he stalled.

Colt studied him. "I understand your way of thinking, but I'm not convinced it's the best line of action. Would this Drake still try to abduct Laura? He may believe it's merely a ruse to get him out in the open."

It could be the sheriff was right, but Stan didn't think so.

"I've done some checking," Colt said. "Drake Simmons has never broken the law in his entire life. Not once. Why would someone like that suddenly break one of the biggest laws that will see him jailed for life?" He shook his head. "It doesn't sit right."

Stan had to agree. It didn't ring true for him either, but he had no other suspects. "I understand, I do," he told the sheriff. "Except I don't have any other viable suspects. Laura told me only a handful of people knew about her father's death, and Simmons was one of them. In fact, from what she said, it was Simmons who suggested the secrecy."

Colt ran a hand across his unshaven chin. "That does sound suspicious," he said quietly.

It was only moments later and there was pounding on the door again. This time when Stan glanced through the glass pane, it made his heart happy. "Come in, come in," he said excitedly, then locked the door again. "Sheriff Colt Turner, meet Cade Anderson." The two men shook hands, then the three headed inside.

~*~

They found Laura in the kitchen. She was wearing one of the new gowns he'd requested and looked far more relaxed than when she wore his oversized nightshirt.

The stew was bubbling on the stove, and she was now cleaning up. She had a large bowl on the countertop, along with flour and a few other ingredients. Was she making bread?

She spun around as they entered the room.

"Laura, meet my friend, Cade Anderson." She glanced first at Stan, then Cade. Lastly, she noticed Colt and smiled.

Cade reached out a hand, and Laura did the same. Then her eyes roamed all over him. Stan knew what she was doing – assessing if he was trustworthy. Her eyes stalled when she noticed the edge of Cade's gun. It was tucked under his jacket, and barely visible.

She never missed a thing. Still, if he was in the same situation, Stan would do exactly the same. Details matter. They can be the difference between life and death.

"Nice to meet you," Cade said.

Everyone loved Cade. He was that sort of person. Personality plus. Except Cade had the same Texas drawl Stan had. He wondered how long it would take Laura to realize.

Not long, apparently. Her smile fell away, and she glared at Stan. Not one for holding back her thoughts, he waited for it. The barrage of words that were sure to come.

One, two, three…

"When are you going to tell me the truth?" she snapped, now facing Stan. She picked up a spoon and stirred the stew. Perhaps agitated was a more appropriate description. She pulled down mugs and slammed them on the countertop.

It was a wonder none of them smashed. Cade glanced at him, the start of a smile on his face. He quickly fought it back.

"I know you are law enforcement." She snapped again, although this time it seemed to be combined with a growl. "Both of you, I'm guessing." She went back to the mugs and filled them with coffee. Except her own, which she filled with tea.

Instead of allowing her to slam them down on the kitchen table and risk burning someone, Stan carried them to their recipients. Laura rummaged through the cupboards until she found a tin that was filled with cookies. She stared at him but said nothing. Instead, she placed them on a plate and took it to the table.

She sat down and sipped her tea, not saying anything. Was she trying to use his tactics now? The thought made him chuckle.

"What's so funny?" She ground out. This was not going as well as Stan had planned, but he knew if he let her seethe for a little longer, Laura might calm down enough to talk to her sensibly.

Or not.

Silence filled the room.

Laura hugged her mug of tea and took a mouthful of the hot beverage. Her eyes scanned the faces of the three men and rested on Stan. He lifted his mug, then put it back down again. He opened his mouth to speak, then thought the better of it.

She was already angry. Perhaps he should let her calm down before telling her the full story. Her eyes pierced him, and he felt even more compelled to tell her everything. Stan stood. "Would you excuse us for a few minutes?" he asked the two men who sat silently. If he were in their boots, Stan would do the exact same thing.

When he glanced at her again, Laura was glaring at him. He couldn't help how she felt in this moment, but once he explained…

She was so riled up it might not make a difference, but he could only try.

Chapter Nine

Laura was incredibly angry with Stan. Had he lied to her from the first moment they met? Almost from the start she'd suspected he wasn't the stonemason he portrayed himself to be. Except…it was not a skill you could pretend to have. Either you knew what you were doing, or you didn't.

The piece Stan was working on when she arrived was the work of a master craftsman. She'd only caught a glance of it, but it was enough to convince her. Now it seemed he was something else altogether.

She still held the mug of tea and sipped it as she sat close to the fire. Stan made a point of adding logs to the fire, although Laura was certain they weren't necessary. It was a ploy, pure and simple. He was putting off what needed to be said.

Finally, he stood. He sat opposite her, in the chair she'd come to know as his. Although truth be known, the place she occupied was his. Until she'd intruded on his life.

Stan picked up the mug of coffee he'd discarded to refuel the fire. He sipped it, clearly putting off what he was now compelled to tell her.

"You're right," he told her, his eyes searching the coffee and not Laura. "I…" His eyes suddenly darted up and stared into hers. "I was a lawman. Texas Ranger." He let out a huge sigh as thought it was a relief to get it off his chest.

Instead of answering, Laura sipped her tea and waited for him to explain himself. "I was born and bred in Texas. My father was a stonemason and planned for me to follow in his footsteps. He trained me from the minute I was old enough to use the tools without drawing blood."

A look of sadness overtook him then, and Laura wanted nothing more than to hold him close and hug away the memories that caused him pain.

After my mother died, I couldn't bear to stay in the house I grew up in. The pull to become a lawman had been there for as long as I could remember. Except…" He took a deep breath.

"You didn't want to let your father down." Laura understood family commitment. Isn't that exactly what she'd done her entire life?

"You got it," he said quietly. "I left, and pursued the one thing my heart told me I needed to do."

Now she was confused. "Except you're not." She studied him. Something obviously happened to change his mind.

"I was a Texas Ranger for nearly two decades. And I was good at what I did. When my father became ill a couple of years ago, I went on a leave of absence to be with him." Stan's voice wavered. It was clear what was coming next.

Laura wanted to go to him. To hold him and tell him everything would be alright. Except she knew he needed to get the words out to move past the pain he felt.

"By that time, my father had semi-retired. He moved to Montana and set up shop here." He glanced about. "This workshop is far smaller than the one he had in Texas. It gave him the opportunity to slow down."

She didn't need to hear the rest. He couldn't bear to leave and instead, stayed here in his father's home. Trying to make up for lost time. Laura knew as well as Stan did, it would never work.

"Being a stonemason is a far slower pace than I ever had as a Texas Ranger. Don't get me wrong, I love law enforcement. And I'm good at it."

He clearly was – she'd seen it firsthand. "But you didn't go back after your father died."

Stan placed his mug of coffee on the side table. It would be cold by now, just as Laura's tea was. "Thank you for explaining," she whispered, then stood. Stan stood too. They were so close, and she couldn't help herself.

Laura wrapped her arms around him and grief overtook her. For two lost fathers. Stan's and hers. They were both orphans and alone. Right now, they only had each other.

To begin with, Stan was rigid. He didn't say anything, nor did he move. She tucked her head against his chest. His heart beat rapidly – whether it was because he'd shared his story or because she held him, Laura would never know.

Slowly, his arms came up and he wrapped them around her. Loosely at first, but then he held her tight. His heart rate slowed down. Laura's did too.

They were like two peas in a pod. Both lonely, both past their prime, but strong in their own way.

Now the truth was out, things could only get better from here. Laura had to believe it was true.

It felt as though they'd stood in each other's arms for a lifetime, but Laura knew it could only be mere minutes. She'd felt a connection with Stan from almost the first moment they'd met. They were soon to be married, and Laura wondered if anything about their relationship would change.

She shook herself mentally. The only *relationship* they had was surface deep. They were not in love, and never would be. This was merely about stopping her kidnapper getting his hands on her father's wealth by force. Nothing more, and nothing less.

Glancing up at him, Stan seemed dazed. As though he hadn't thought about what he was doing and now regretted it. "We shouldn't…I'm sorry," he said, then let his arms drop to his sides.

Stepping back, Laura knew it was her fault and not his. "Not at all," she whispered. "My fault entirely."

He studied her, but didn't say another word. Not immediately anyway. He simply continued to gaze at her. Until he lifted a hand and caressed her cheek. A shiver ran down Laura's spine at his gentle touch. "We should get back with the others," he said, dropping his hand.

"Of course," Laura said agreeably, despite the fact she'd rather stay here with him. Just the two of them.

She shuddered.

Laura knew she couldn't think this way. Later that day they would be married. The marriage would be in name only, and only for show. There was one reason and one reason only for this happening – to stop her abductor stealing her family fortune. If she was already married, he couldn't touch her.

It was surely his plan. It was the only thing that made sense. He would marry Laura, then take what would be rightfully his in the eyes of the law. It would mean the end of her independence, and likely her family's legacy. She didn't know a whole lot about Drake, except he'd worked as her father's assistant for many years. He was diligent in his work and had always had both her father's best interest at heart, as well as the business as a whole.

Why he had turned against her at this extremely difficult time, Laura didn't know. She did understand her marriage to Stan should be treated as a matter of urgency. "What time are we getting married?" she asked as they stood close to each other.

Stan reached for her hand. "You look confused. Or is that determination I see?" He chuckled, but suddenly turned serious. "You're worried, aren't you? What do you think will happen?"

"This is way out of character for Drake. I said from the start I wasn't convinced he was involved, and I still feel that way." Her heart hammered.

"If not Drake, then who?" Stan studied her again. If he was looking to Laura for an answer, he would be sadly disappointed.

She had absolutely no idea.

Chapter Ten

Stan was certain Drake was the culprit. Except Laura now had him wondering.

The man was an office assistant, and little more. He likely ran errands for his wealthy employer, or perhaps he had people under him who did that. It was highly unlikely Laura would have complete knowledge of how her father's office was run.

There were few people he would pin her kidnapping on. Only a handful were even aware Joseph Hartley had died. He had ruled out the undertaker and everyone involved with Hartley's burial. According to Laura, they had been paid handsomely to keep quiet.

Laura had made fresh coffee and was now attending to the stew. She punched the bread, then set it aside again. Even as he silently went over the details of this case, his eyes drifted to the woman who would soon be his wife. Even in her time of despair she was more capable than most people he knew.

"Laura," he said firmly. "Come and sit down. I need to ask you something."

She turned to face him, and didn't look pleased. As she stepped toward the table, Stan realized it wasn't that she was displeased. Laura was exhausted and distressed about everything that had happened and was still happening.

They had to stop the man who was trying to kidnap her. And they needed to do it sooner than later. Her life depended on it.

She sat quietly and sipped her tea while she waited for him to ask his question.

"Tell me about your father's office. The hierarchy." Not really a question, but it was important.

Frowning, Laura gazed at him. She shook her head, then answered. "Drake was Father's assistant. He did all the difficult stuff, including the ledgers. He typically had staff below him do all the menial work."

"Such as?"

Laura studied him for mere moments. "There were two women and one man in the office. The women mostly did typing, making coffee, bringing lunch for both Father and Drake. That sort of thing."

"And the man?" Stan wondered if Laura even knew what he did. Nor did he believe she could name each person.

He glanced across the table. Cade and the sheriff both leaned in, ensuring they heard all the details.

"I don't believe I ever met him," Laura said, curiosity in her voice. She tapped the table with her fingers. She rolled her eyes, then closed them. Clearly, she was trying to recall something and was having trouble.

He kept quiet, as did the others. This could be crucial information, so they would give her time and space.

"You have to remember," she said, her eyes now focused on Stan. "I didn't visit the office very often. I did a lot of charity work, and it filled my time."

"Didn't you tell me your father started training you to take over the business?" Stan was certain it was what she'd said.

"I did, except it wasn't often. Drake assured me what I didn't learn from Father, he could teach me." She licked her lips and rolled her shoulders. "He understood how upsetting it was for me having to learn the business. We both knew it was Father planning for his death."

Her eyes filled with unshed tears, and Laura turned her face away. She suddenly pushed her chair back, scraping it across the floor. Stirring the stew again, she kept her back to them all. Stan wanted to go to her, hold her, and make everything alright again, but knew he shouldn't.

They were already becoming too familiar, and he wondered how they would be once they were man and wife.

Her shoulders shook, and Stan was certain she was crying. His biggest wish right now was the other two men were not here. If they were alone, he would go to her. He would hold Laura against him and let her cry for as long and hard as she wanted.

Except he knew she would be annoyed if he did that. In her mind, it would cause her embarrassment. Well, damnabbit, he was going to do it anyway.

He pushed his chair back quickly, causing it to grate across the floor and through him. The two lawmen sitting at the table stared at him with open mouths. Stan indicated for them to leave. To get out of the room.

He didn't care where they went. He simply wanted them gone. Wanted privacy for the woman who was about to become his wife. Pretend or not, he owed it to Laura to care for her. If that meant holding her in times of distress, then so be it.

The moment Cade and Colt left the room, he went to Laura. She startled as he touched her shoulder, then leaned back into him when she realized it was her soon-to-be-husband standing behind her.

She put down the ladle she'd been using to stir the stew, and his arms wrapped around her. "It will all work out," he whispered in her ear.

She shook her head. "I don't think it will. I don't care about the money. Drake can have it all as far as I'm concerned," she said quietly. "I only care about the family legacy. To ensure it continues as it has already done for generations. Father felt the same."

Stan was shocked by her words. Especially the part where Joseph Hartley felt the same way. Had he been training Drake to take over the business? Or perhaps he was going to install Drake as manager but hadn't made it official.

Both scenarios rang true for Stan. "Did your father plan on Drake taking over?" He felt Laura stiffen in his arms.

"Not that I'm aware of. But he would not have necessarily told me if he wanted to do so." She turned in his arms and stared up into Stan's face. "Do you think that's the motivation for my kidnapping? To get what Father promised him?"

Stan gently wiped away her tears. "I don't know, but it could well be."

Laura studied him. She was good at that – every time she did, it felt like she was gazing into his soul. "It's an excellent idea. If it turns out not to be Drake, I will appoint him manager. He'll get a big, fat, salary, and I won't have to worry about the business."

Her words surprised Stan. "He's that good?"

"My father said he is. Joseph Hartley's opinion is good enough for me."

What she didn't voice was the part where Drake couldn't be her kidnapper if he wanted the job.

Stan didn't blame her one iota.

Chapter Eleven

Laura's heart pounded as she stood in Stan's arms. Each time they stood together like this, the more comfortable she became.

Resting her head against his chest, Laura thought about their conversation. "If not Drake, then who?" she asked quietly, then glanced up at Stan.

He frowned. He'd discussed Drake as though he was definitely her kidnapper. Laura wasn't convinced. It wasn't that she knew Drake as much as her father did, but felt she knew him enough that it wasn't in his character to behave in such a way.

Stan shifted slightly, and she studied him. His hand came up and Laura tilted her face. His hand cupped her cheek.

Neither one of them should engage in this sort of behavior, and they both knew it.

Their eyes met, and Stan dropped his hand away. It wasn't what Laura wanted, and yet it was. The more time they spent together, the closer they seemed to become. She rested her head on his chest again, but only momentarily.

They really must not act in this way. The fact they were about to get married did not forgive either of them. It was a fake marriage, a ruse, meant to stop one action – her kidnapper stealing the Hartley Family fortune.

"Who is looking after the business?"

Stan's voice shook Laura out of her thoughts. She frowned. "I…I don't know. I left Drake to take over until all the paperwork was sorted by our lawyer."

Without warning, Stan's hands held her by the arms. He frowned momentarily, apologized, then stormed away.

Heart pounding, Laura turned back to the stove and stirred the stew. What had made Stan suddenly agitated? She went over the conversation in her mind. There wasn't anything she could think of to cause him to leave like that.

She added wood to the cookstove and prepared the tins for the bread. Laura still didn't know how many mouths she would be feeding tonight, but there would be plenty no matter how many turned up.

Nothing would surprise her. Stan was one big surprise after another much of the time. Laura wasn't sure she would ever get used to it.

After greasing the bread tins, she put them aside, then pounded the bread dough. It was ready for cooking. Laura cut the dough in half and placed each half in the tins. After adding them to the oven, she felt lost. There was little for her to do now, except sit around and wait for the preacher to arrive.

Laura sat next to the fire and kept warm. The men were in the kitchen, chatting. She couldn't hear what they were saying, despite wanting to know. She shrugged her shoulders – she would find out soon enough.

After what seemed like forever, she stood. Laura needed to stir the stew. It wouldn't do to burn their supper. As she stood, Stan entered the room.

"Change of plans," he said, then reached for her hand. "We're going to the church to get married. If we do it here, your kidnapper won't know you are no longer unattached."

What he said was true. But was it safe?

As if he could read her mind, Stan put her at ease. "He won't get to you. You will have two Texas Rangers and a sheriff flanking you. If he's available, the sheriff's deputy will be there, too."

Laura nodded, although she wasn't convinced his plan would work. "What time?" she asked. She had already learned when Stan made up his mind it couldn't be changed.

"Is ten minutes long enough?" The grin on his face told her he was trying to coerce Laura into getting ready quickly. She wanted to get it over and done with as quickly as he did. Except she needed to change into the gown she'd been given for this very reason. Her hair needed to be brushed and put up, and she had to wash her face.

Laura was certain she must look an absolute mess. "I'll do my best, but can't guarantee ten minutes is enough," she told him.

He pulled a face she couldn't decipher. Men did strange things sometimes. Laura wasn't sure she would ever work them out.

Laura headed toward the bedroom she was already sharing with her husband-to-be. Not that she was given a choice. She'd been placed there by Stan. Laura had to admit she felt safer with him nearby. He said it was his only motivation, and she had no choice but to believe him.

She changed out of her day dress and into the fancy gown that had been chosen for this purpose. It would double as her Sunday best, except Laura knew she wouldn't be allowed to attend church. And more likely, would be confined to Stan's home.

At least it would be the case until her kidnapper was caught.

How long it would be her home, Laura wasn't sure. What she did know was she liked to get out and spend time with other people. Her charity work especially had her socializing with people who were far worse off than Laura.

She genuinely wanted to help people, and her father's wealth allowed her to do that. Laura pulled herself up. It was now *her* wealth. Soon to legally be Stan's wealth. This wasn't a ruse Stan planned to obtain her fortune. Stan wasn't like that. She truly believed he was marrying her to protect Laura from whoever was trying to get her fortune.

Who that person was, worried her. If Drake was the kidnapper, who was keeping the business afloat?

Fully dressed and almost ready to go, she opened the bedroom door. Stan was pacing the floor, waiting for her.

She motioned for him to come closer. He frowned. Did he think she had changed her mind? It wasn't like she had a lot of choice. "Come closer," she whispered, and he leaned down. When she whispered again, he stood straight and grinned.

"Turn around," he told her as he chuckled.

"Not out here!" she said, exasperated. That would never do – the other men were standing nearby.

They moved into the bedroom, and Stan half closed the bedroom door. Laura could still hear the laughter in his voice. His hands gently touched her shoulders, then worked their way down her back. His touch sent a shiver down her spine.

"How many buttons has this dress got?" he asked, clearly frustrated.

She clucked. "I didn't choose it, so don't blame me," she said firmly. Laura had no intention of admitting she'd enjoyed every moment.

Just as she knew Stan would not admit to it either.

Chapter Twelve

Stan stepped outside his stonemason's workshop onto the street. He glanced about. It was quiet, almost too quiet.

Harrietville wasn't exactly a small town, but it wasn't huge either. There was usually a handful of people about, but the street was void of any movement. He wasn't sure if it was merely coincidental, or someone had caused everyone to stay inside.

Surely if there had been some kind of incident, they'd know about it?

He rolled his shoulders, then glanced about again. This time, a customer came out of the mercantile, and another went inside. The door to the diner opened, and the bootmaker stood outside his store. The man sat on a chair outside the door and lit up a cigarette. Quiet day, Stan guessed.

"All clear," he said firmly, and the other men stepped forward. They all fell into position, and Laura was quickly surrounded. Stan waited until he heard the click of the lock, then squeezed Laura's hand.

He stood to her left, the other three men covered each position possible to ensure she was protected. They wanted the kidnapper to see her, but not to shoot her. Although Stan had already suspected killing her was not on the man's agenda. If she was dead, he couldn't get his hands on her fortune.

It was the thing that convinced him to go ahead with this plan.

He felt the terror that ran through her body. She was shaking so badly, she could barely walk. He wasn't surprised when she stumbled. Stan put an arm around her waist, and supported his soon-to-be-wife. "We're almost there," he whispered, then glanced about again. The street was again clear.

They hurried inside the church the moment they arrived. Stan was relieved despite not expecting trouble. He never left anything to chance. He would not have lasted so long as a Texas Ranger had he done so.

He locked the church's main door the moment they entered. Cade began to search for any unwanted visitors. "All clear," he called.

They headed down to the front of the church, where Preacher Leonard Nichols waited. The sheriff's deputy stood nearby, ensuring no harm came to the preacher.

A smile came to the preacher's lips. "Welcome, everyone," he said warmly. Introductions were made, and soon the ceremony was underway. It wasn't long before Stan was signing the marriage certificate, and Miss Laura Hartley was now Mrs. Stanley Munro.

He breathed a huge sigh of relief, but Stan knew his wife's ordeal wasn't over. Her kidnapper was still out there somewhere.

The problem he had now, apart from protecting his wife, was to discover who was behind all this. Was it Drake Simmons, or someone else entirely?

Stan shook himself mentally. His job, his only job right now, was to ensure the safety of his bride. He needed to get her back home without incident, but he also wanted to buy whatever essentials she required.

Two gowns did not make a wardrobe of clothes, and she surely needed more essentials. "We need to make a stop before we go back home," Stan announced.

Cade gazed at him, but didn't seem surprised. "Where are we going?"

"To the mercantile. My wife needs clothes." His words were firm. No one was left believing this was a suggestion. He glanced at Laura. Her cheeks were bright red. She was embarrassed. For what reason?

Stan was not used to having a woman around, especially not a wife.

"Thank you, Lenny," Stan told the preacher. "We appreciate it." He then turned toward the back of the church and headed down the aisle. Cade unlocked the door, then gazed up and down the street.

The mercantile was diagonally opposite the church. It wouldn't take long to get there, and his wife was still well protected. "All clear," Cade announced, and they all stepped outside.

Laura was no longer shaking. The motivation for her kidnapping had been taken away. She was married, and the kidnapper, whoever it may be, could no longer claim Laura's fortune.

"I really don't need anything," she said quietly.

Stan's eyes left the street for mere moments. He couldn't afford to let his guard down. "Yes you do," he said firmly. Moments later they were inside the mercantile. It was thoroughly searched before the mercantile owner's wife led Laura to the back of the store. Stan was only a few steps behind.

"Let me check your size," Jennifer Irving said, and ran her eyes over Laura. "Oh! I recognize this gown. The preacher's wife bought it recently." She smiled. "The pale blue color really suits you." She lifted a gown from the rack and held it in front of Laura. "This one would work too." Jennifer pulled out several gowns and held them in front of the new bride. "How many do you need?"

"None," Laura said tightly.

"At least three," Stan said firmly. "She needs everything – nightgowns, stockings, unmen…" he stopped then. He couldn't even say the word, let alone look at the items on the shelf.

Jennifer smiled broadly. "Don't you worry, Stanley. I have it all in hand."

He flinched at her use of his full name. No one called him Stanley. Not now. His mother called him that when she was cross with him, but that was such a long time ago.

"It's too much," Laura said. "Besides, I have my own money."

Indeed, she did, and Stan knew it. Except no wife of his would pay for anything. It wasn't as though he couldn't afford it. He rarely spent money except for supplies of stone. "So do I," he said firmly. He sounded far heavy handed than he'd intended. "Get everything you need." His words too, were forceful. It wasn't the way he conducted himself.

Jennifer stared at him. Her eyes then drifted to Laura. "Do you need time to sort this out?" she asked, clearly ready to leave them alone.

"Not at all," Stan said, this time his voice gentle.

Laura threw her hands up in the air. "You win," she said, sounding frustrated and deflated.

It was the right thing to do, Stan knew it was. He was her husband and was responsible for her in every way. He was happy for things to be that way.

So why did his heart feel like it had shattered?

Chapter Thirteen

Laura balked at the large box of clothing and other items Stan had bought for her. He also gave her a bouquet of flowers. No one had ever done that before.

On second thought, they had. When she turned twenty-one and could then access her trust fund, a trail of would-be suitors turned up. Some arrived with flowers, others with boxes of candy. The truly serious suitors arrived with both.

None were happy when she turned them all away.

Neither the flowers nor the candies appeased her. Laura simply wasn't interested in marriage. Not one of those men had bothered with her before. They appeared at the most inappropriate times. They turned up at dances she was forced to attend, and then when she became of age.

Flowers, candy, and the men carrying them. They meant absolutely nothing to Laura. But this – Stan presenting her with flowers – it was different. It meant a lot.

She put the flowers to her face and breathed in the fragrance. The beauty of them, and the enticing scent, changed her mood. She had been angry. Frustrated at being coerced into something she didn't want. Except she had to do it to save her life.

When Stan told her what he believed to be the kidnappers plan, she didn't believe him. She found it extremely difficult to believe someone would kidnap, marry, then kill her. Now though, after listening to Stan and the other lawmen, she was convinced.

Except Laura still refused to believe Drake was behind all this. On the few occasions she'd seen him in her father's office, Drake was nothing but a gentleman. She even thought, on a day she'd let her guard down, they may have had a future together. Father was certainly pushing her toward it.

He'd even said marrying Drake would solve a lot of problems. It would mean the business would be well looked after for generations to come.

"I need to tell you something," Laura told Stan quietly. "It's important." She brought the flowers back up to her face and breathed in the luxurious fragrance. Curiosity filled his face, but Stan didn't push her to tell him now.

Instead, he reached for the box containing her clothes, and the food supplies Laura requested.

Today had been somewhat of a trial. She could only hope things got better.

~*~

"It wasn't Drake." Laura was adamant, yet Stan didn't seem to agree.

Everyone sat at the kitchen table, coffee in their hands. Laura stared down into her tea, waiting for a response from Stan. Instead, he studied her. "Is that what you wanted to tell me?" He seemed a little annoyed. Perhaps her new husband believed what she planned to tell him was groundbreaking. Except it wasn't.

"There's more to it," she said gruffly. "I remembered a conversation my father repeated practically every time I visited him at his office."

Stan sat patiently waiting for the details. Seemingly not so annoyed this time. He didn't speak, just sat there gazing at her.

"He decided I should marry Drake. He had discussed it several times."

Stan's eyes opened wide. He seemed shocked at the revelation. "With Drake there? What did he think about it?"

Laura thought back to the conversations they'd had over the past several months. "At first, Drake wasn't interested at all. After a while he gave in to Father's demands." Laura couldn't help herself. She grimaced.

"The thing that stopped it going anywhere was my objection. I told Father that just because he was Joseph Hartley, he did not get to control me or my life." Now Laura felt cross. Almost as much as she did at the time.

Stan leaned closer to her. "What did Drake say? Or do?"

Laura shrugged her shoulders. "Very little. He gazed at me, then told my father he wouldn't forcibly marry me." She huffed. "As if either of them had a choice."

As he tried to force back a grin, Laura felt her annoyance becoming anger. She took a mouthful of her tea and slammed the mug down on the table. Laura shocked even herself. The lawmen sitting nearby raised their eyebrows but didn't say anything.

The stew needed stirring and she had to check on the bread.

Their supper was coming along nicely, although Laura had never stirred stew so vigorously. She sensed her husband behind her, rather than knew he was there. His hands came down on her shoulders, and he leaned in.

"I apologize," he whispered in her ear. Laura wasn't sure how she could be mad at this man, and yet she was.

She stepped back, forcing Stan to move back also. Grabbing two kitchen towels, she opened the oven door. She pulled one bread tin out and placed it on the countertop. Laura tapped the top of the loaf. It sounded hollow. "Perfect," she said, then leaned in and reached for the second bread tin. She tipped the bread out of both tins and placed them on a chopping board to cool.

The kitchen smelled divine. She'd done little cooking since Father passed, choosing instead to go to a local restaurant. "Drake came with me," she mumbled. Another fact she'd forgotten.

She stirred the stew again, although in reality, it was totally unnecessary.

"Drake went with you where?" Cade's voice penetrated her thoughts, and Laura turned to face him.

"To the restaurant. He said…" She stopped and thought for a moment. "He said it wasn't safe for me to be out at night alone." She laughed then. A bitter sound, even to her own ears. "As it turned out, being home at night and alone wasn't safe either."

"He left you alone?" Stan seemed very interested in what she had to say.

Laura sighed. "I told him to go. It wouldn't look right for him to stay in the house with me when there was no chaperone."

Stan frowned.

"People talk. Especially in a place like Helena. We would be forced to marry, and that's not something I was prepared to do."

Stan opened his mouth to speak, but slammed it shut again. Laura knew what he was thinking – it's exactly what they'd done today. They barely knew each other. She had known Drake for much longer yet wouldn't marry him. Even knowing it was her father's greatest wish.

She rolled her eyes. "I do understand the irony of it. Only I really had no choice this time."

Pounding on the door had Laura retreating to the sitting room. She was surrounded by law enforcement officers, and she needed time to herself. Near the fire she felt calm and relaxed. At least most of the time.

If anything else happened, she was away from it all. She leaned back in the chair and let the warmth of the fire wash over her.

Chapter Fourteen

Stan hurried to the door, gun at the ready. Cade was two steps behind him, with his gun drawn as well.

Glancing through the glass panel, Stan recognized his former colleague, Tommy Flanagan. He was pleased the Texas Rangers had come through for him. Despite his long absence.

Stan unlocked the door and ushered Tommy inside. "Good to see you," he said, shaking hands with the newcomer. "Thanks for coming."

Tommy studied him. "Of course I came. You need help, I got here as quickly as I could." He reached across and shook Cade's hand. "Looks like the team is back together," Tommy added.

Those days were long gone, and they all knew it. They were a good team though, and Stan couldn't deny it. "Let's go inside," Stan said as he locked the door.

"What exactly has happened," Tommy asked, with no idea how complicated this had become. They hurried into the cottage.

With Laura asleep by the fire, they could talk openly. Stan stirred the stew in Laura's absence, then poured coffee for Tommy. The others refused the offer.

Explaining Laura's situation to Tommy was difficult. Far more difficult than Stan ever imagined it could be. At first, he was on the outside looking in. Now he was on the inside and Laura was his legal wife. Even if it was only for show – to stop her kidnapper marrying her and stealing Laura's fortune.

"At the start, I believed Drake Simmons, the father's assistant, was the culprit."

Tommy interrupted. "But now you don't?"

"Not at all," Stan said. He rubbed a hand over his chin. "According to Laura, he was protective of her after her father died. Took her to dinner and advised her not to stay home alone. She refused his advice, and the rest you know."

"Go on," Tommy said. "I can tell there's more."

"It appears Drake isn't in love with her and refused to marry Laura against her will." This was the part Stan couldn't comprehend. If he was adamant, he wouldn't force Laura when her father was alive, he surely wouldn't do so after he died.

"Right," Tommy said. "We've rule Drake out as the culprit. Who are your other suspects?"

Stan rolled his shoulders trying to relieve the stiffness. "We have none." He knew it sounded bad, but it was the truth of the matter. "Joseph Hartley's death has not been announced publicly. Only a handful of people are aware of the situation."

"Including Drake," Cade said firmly. Stan gazed at him. Cade still believed Drake was Laura's abductor.

Tommy glanced from one to the other. "Let's settle this now." He turned to Colt. "Sheriff, I need your assistance."

Stan gawked. He couldn't help himself. "What are you up to?" Tommy had always been a bit of a lone wolf. Stan recalled other times when Tommy had a theory and disappeared to follow a trail.

"Of course," the sheriff said. "Ready when you are."

The sheriff and the newcomer stood. "The only way to rule Drake out is to check his whereabouts. It's exactly what I'm about to do," Tommy said.

Furious with himself for not thinking of it himself, Stan walked with them to the door. He locked it securely behind the pair, then headed back inside.

Once again, he stirred the stew. It wouldn't do for it to burn after all the work Laura put into it. Then he checked on his new wife. She was still sound asleep in the sitting room. He leaned in and kissed her forehead, then silently admonished himself.

Their marriage was fake, and he had to keep his distance.

He would keep telling himself, but standing there, looking down at her, Stan saw her vulnerability. She might be a strong woman, but she was in an extremely difficult situation. Her strength was diminishing before his very eyes.

Not wanting to leave her alone, although she slept, Stan had no choice but to return to the kitchen. He needed to work out a suspect list.

There weren't too many people involved. Which meant it should be easy. Except it wasn't. He had no idea who each of the suspects were. It was something he'd have to find out, even if it meant leaving Laura alone for a day or two to find out. She would have several lawman surrounding her and would be safe.

For some unfathomable reason, Stan despised that option. He would send one of his Texas Ranger friends instead.

~*~

Naming suspects was more difficult than Stan imagined.

There was of course, Drake Simmons. Even though Laura was adamant it wasn't Drake who kidnapped her.

There were only a handful of other suspects – the doctor who attended to Joseph Hartley and signed the death certificate, the undertaker, his assistant, and the grave diggers.

According to Laura, they were all paid handsomely for their silence, so why they would then kidnap her, he had no idea. Except Stan had learned over the years that criminals were highly unpredictable.

As he wrote each person's occupation, he realized it was a lost cause. Without actual names, how was he expected to investigate each of those people? He suspected even Laura may not be able to help.

The one person who likely could assist him, was high on Stan's suspect list. Asking Drake for the information was putting him on alert. If he was the guilty party, he could cover his tracks and ensure he wasn't implicated.

Stan was missing something; he was certain of it. He also knew he was too close to the victim. Laura. His wife.

He shook himself mentally. Their marriage was fake. There was no emotion involved from either party. He'd only married Laura to save her from the kidnapper. And she only married him for the safety it provided.

The moment it was all over, they would apply for an annulment and go back to their own lives. Stan knew it, and so did Laura.

So why did the mere thought of it make him feel miserable?

Chapter Fifteen

By the time Laura awoke, it was getting late. The fire was still burning brightly, and Stan sat in the chair opposite.

He was staring at her. It made Laura wonder how long he'd been sitting there watching her every move.

"Did you sleep well?" he asked, making small talk. If he'd watched her for any length of time, Stan would surely know she'd barely moved. Sitting on these chairs was extremely comfortable. Sleeping on them, was an entirely different story.

She stretched herself out, trying to remove the kinks from staying in the one position for so long. "I did," Laura said. "Remind me not to fall asleep on these chairs again."

Stan grimaced. Did he think it was his fault she was aching? "Oh!" she said, finally properly awake. "Supper will be ruined." Her disappointment was overwhelming.

"It's fine," Stan told her. "I've kept a check on it."

Laura was more relieved than she thought she would be. She'd put a lot of work into making the stew, and she certainly didn't want it to burn. Thankfully she'd made the bread earlier. Fresh bread with freshly cooked stew was a favorite of hers, and she was fairly certain it would be with Stan too.

The moment she stood, Stan followed. He put a hand to her waist and guided her toward the kitchen. "I need to ask you some questions," he said quietly. "If you feel up to it."

Laura gazed at him. "Am I able to do that while I see to the supper?" She went straight to the woodstove and checked the stew. Stan had done a good job of ensuring it didn't stick.

"That should work," her new husband said, then sat at the table. "I need the names of the people involved with your father's death and burial." He lifted his hand and held it ready to write.

Laura let out a long and meaningful sigh. "That's the one thing I can't help you with. Except for Father's physician. Doctor Fenwick Thorne. He treated my father for at least a decade. Longer, in fact." She reached up to pull down dinner plates but couldn't reach. Stan was by her side before Laura could even ask for help. She smiled briefly, then continued. "There is one person who will know for certain, and that's Drake. Why don't you give him a call?"

She could tell by the expression on Stan's face, it was not something he intended to do. Laura knew the reason why – he still believed it was Drake who kidnapped her. "It wasn't Drake," she said firmly, then turned away from him. "If it had been, I wouldn't have been afraid."

That was the crux of the matter. Until now, Laura hadn't admitted what she'd known all along. It truly wasn't Drake. "This food is ready. How long before the sheriff will be back?"

"Should be soon. Plus, another ranger. Tommy." He scribbled down the information Laura had provided, but Laura knew he was so focused on Drake, Stan did not want to admit it could be someone else, and in reality, was another man.

"Drake has been so kind and caring toward me since Father passed," she said firmly. "He has ensured I was never alone outside of the house and tried to arrange security for the house." She brushed some loose hair back behind her ears. "As it turned out, I should have listened to him."

Laura didn't expect Stan to answer, but was convinced he would agree with her. Had she taken Drake's advice, none of this would have happened. Had she listened, she would be in her own home, enjoying her own peace and quiet.

She certainly wouldn't be in a strange town, married to a man she barely knew. Not that she could complain. Stan had been nothing but kind and protective toward her.

Pounding on the door startled Laura.

Stan stood. "It will be the sheriff and Tommy," he said.

Laura shuddered as she noticed Stan pull his gun from its holster. Of course, she knew it was dangerous work he did, but seeing a firearm in his hands brought it home.

What she would have done if Stan had rejected her, Laura didn't know. Those first few minutes had been crucial. Had it been someone else who found her, she may have been killed. Shot as a trespasser when she was trying to save her life.

A shiver went down her spine.

Cade stood. "I'll go," he said, and Stan replaced the gun in his holster.

She had been so focused on Stan and their discussion, she hadn't even noticed Cade in the room.

~*~

Tommy reached for another slice of bread. "You are an excellent cook. It is the best meal I've had for a very long time," he said, waving a hand about the table.

Stan chuckled. "You still cooking for yourself?"

It was clear to Laura it was a joke between the three lawmen – Stan, Cade, and Tommy. They all chuckled, but the sheriff appeared bewildered.

Laura jumped up from the table and checked the oven. Using a kitchen cloth, she removed the pie from the oven. "Anyone for more stew?" She knew even before asking at least some of them would opt for seconds.

All four plates were pushed forward. Laura forced herself not to chuckle. She filled the plates, then cut the apple pie into equal sized pieces. The bowls were filled, and the cream placed in the middle of the table.

While the men finished off their second round of stew, she cleared whatever soiled plates were hers for the taking. The moment the first course was finished, Stan's head shot up. "Something smells delicious," he said, glancing about.

"Everything smells delicious," Tommy said. "You have caught yourself a good one." The moment the words were out, he looked guilty. "Sorry, Laura. No offense intended."

Stan glared at his friend. Moments later Tommy yelped. "What did you do that for?" he demanded of Stan.

"Because you have a big mouth." Stan was fuming.

Laura hadn't seen him this angry before. Was he defending her? Is that what it was all about? It was no longer playful banter between friends. Stan was seriously annoyed.

"Stan," she said loudly. "It is fine. No offense taken." Laura turned to Tommy and smiled. She wanted him to know his words had not upset her. Not even a little bit.

She collected up all the soiled dishes and placed them in the sink. Once done, she distributed the desserts. As suspected, the men tucked into their desserts. "Just so you know, there are no seconds. I cut the pie to give you each a larger piece."

They each looked up and grinned, then went back to their food. Laura felt a strange satisfaction knowing she had appeased these men and filled their bellies.

She sat down at the table with them and ate her own dessert. If she did say so herself, it was good. Laura could see more baking coming up in her future.

Chapter Sixteen

Stan, along with the others, retreated to the sitting room. It wasn't that the kitchen was cold, although it was cooler than the sitting room with its far larger fire.

It was more to do with discussing Laura's situation without her hearing about it. Stan believed she had calmed down considerably; hence the reason discussions were held in her presence. Now he believed it to be untrue. She was jumpy, and easily startled. Laura was also convinced Drake was not her kidnapper.

Should he be rethinking his position on Drake as a suspect? He had to wonder.

Tommy sipped his coffee, then addressed the assembled lawmen. "We've been in contact with the sheriff in Helena. He will make enquiries, then get back to me." He took another mouthful of coffee. "Hopefully tomorrow, but I wouldn't count on it," he said.

"Eliminating Drake Simmons, or knowing he is a possible suspect will make our job easier." Stan still wasn't convinced Simmons wasn't involved. He wasn't sure if it was despite Laura's insistence, or because of it. At least they would soon have a better idea whether the man was the kidnapper.

He wouldn't put it past anyone to pretend to care, only to make the victim comfortable around them.

"Something I did manage to find out from the sheriff," Tommy added, "was Drake Simmons made the missing person report about Laura. With no family, the sheriff accepted the report from her father's assistant."

Stan was stunned. Either Simmons was very good at covering his tracks, or he genuinely was not involved in Laura's abduction.

Silence filled the room. Stan was not the only lawman here who had assumed it to be the assistant. Eliminating him would make a huge difference to their investigations.

"Are we to believe Drake Simmons has kept Hartley Textiles running all this time?" It put a whole new perspective on the situation. If her father's assistant had been working at the office all this time, he couldn't have kidnapped Laura.

Unless he had an accomplice.

Tommy studied Stan, who not once took his eyes off his friend. "That's the assumption. I've asked the sheriff to also provide details of Joseph Hartley's will."

Stan now realized he was far too close to the victim in this case. The will should have been one of his priorities, and yet it hadn't been. "I don't suppose you asked him about the other potential suspects?" Stan raised his eyebrows, not expecting it was even on Tommy's agenda.

"Of course. Although Sheriff Boyle suspected it could be difficult information to find. Especially the grave diggers. They are often transient, he told me."

Stan completely understood. Drifters were often given menial jobs, knowing they would quickly move on to another town with potentially better pay. Stan grunted. Nothing about this case was going the way he expected it would.

"Stan," Cade said gently. "You need to step back. Let us do the work. You concentrate on Laura. She needs you."

He grunted again. Did she? Laura seemed to be more than capable. Except Stan knew she couldn't protect herself. As her husband, it was his job. And yet, one of his best friends was telling him to leave it all to them.

Could he do it? Could Stan walk away from this case and spend his time ensuring Laura was both mentally and physically alright?

There was only one way to find out. He mentally pushed back on his main concern – getting too close to Laura. But Stan knew it was already too late. His feelings for her were getting stronger by the day.

~*~

Laura turned as he entered the kitchen. "More coffee?" she asked, but her expression was one of curiosity.

She knew he'd rather be with the other lawmen, discussing her case, and clearly wondered why he was here now. Alone.

"They kicked me off the case," he said gruffly.

She tried to hide her amusement, but he saw it. Her smile was fleeting, but it had been there. "You told me you have been on a leave of absence for some time. What's the problem?"

His heart squeezed and pain went through him. "The problem is you are my wife. I vowed to protect you." Stan dragged a chair from under the table and sat down with a thud.

Again, that fleeting smile. Was she mocking him?

"It doesn't sound like a bad idea to me. You have been focused on Drake, and I know it wasn't him."

Why Laura was so determined on that one point, he had no idea. "Tommy has the Helena sheriff looking into Drake."

"Oh?" She seemed surprised, then shrugged her shoulders. "Sheriff Boyle is a good man. If there's anything to find, he will. Except he won't find anything bad about Drake, I can guarantee it."

Confusion filled Stan. Why was Laura so adamant? He studied her closely. There had to be more to her belief than he could see, but he had no idea what it might be. Questioning her further would be fruitless. He got the same answer every time – it wasn't Drake.

If he assumed Laura was correct, and the obvious suspect wasn't the guilty party, they had few other suspects to look at. Once they had names and backgrounds, the investigation could move forward.

Once they arrested the guilty party, all their lives could go back to normal. Except Stan wasn't sure it was what he wanted.

Did he really want to lose Laura? Their fake marriage felt more real by the hour. The only problem was, she didn't feel the same.

Did she?

Chapter Seventeen

Laura could see Stan was conflicted.

Clearly, he was hurt at being forced out of the investigation. After all, it was Stan who set the ball rolling once she'd arrived in his workshop. It was also Stan who had *interrogated* her until she couldn't take it anymore.

What she couldn't understand was his insistence about Drake's guilt. Although, in his situation she might feel the same way.

Drake was the perfect suspect. He knew how to run the business, and exactly how much it was worth. How much *she* was worth. Each time they'd gone out to dinner after her father's death, he'd insisted on paying. Laura was keenly aware his salary was not pitiful and was aligned with that of a highly paid executive. Simply because that's what Drake was.

Why her father insisted on calling Drake his assistant, Laura didn't know. His worked appeared to be more like that of a financial advisor or general manager than an assistant.

"General manager?" Stan's voice cut into her thoughts, and Laura's head shot up. "Is that what Drake does?" He studied her when she gazed at him, totally confused. "You muttered the words. I didn't catch the rest."

She must be going mad. Laura could have sworn she thought those words, not said them out loud. She had no choice but to give Stan the full story. She sighed. "Drake began as an assistant, but my father saw his potential. In fact, he felt sure Drake had been hiding his true worth for some reason. Over time, he was trained by my father to ensure the business was always viable. No matter what."

"Except no one knew this?"

Laura shook her head. "Father believed it was safer that way. If word got out that Drake was handling all the finances for the company, including dealing with the bank, it could be dangerous. For Drake." She sighed again.

Stan studied her. "Still think he didn't kidnap you?"

"He didn't need to. Honestly, Stan, you are focused on the wrong person. Drake has full access to enough money to last him three lifetimes. Ten lifetimes. More. He has the authority to withdraw every last dollar in the company account. The power to fire and sack people, and far more." Laura felt anger building inside her. "Father decided he was a perfect husband for me, and he was right. Except I refused to be forced into marriage simply because it suited my father's plans for the future."

"And Drake refused to allow you to be forced."

"She's right." Cade's voice drifted across from the doorway. "You are far too focused on Drake Simmons. We, meaning Tommy and I, believe he's being used as a pawn. Whoever the real kidnapper is, wants it to look like Drake was the perpetrator." He pulled out a chair and joined them at the table.

Laura raised her eyebrows. She didn't agree or disagree, and she certainly didn't say *I told you so.*

Stan glared at Cade. "Don't kill the messenger," Cade said. "We all agree Drake is out of the picture. At least for now. Once we hear back from Sheriff Boyle, we'll know for sure."

Laura was certain once Stan was overridden on his opinion about the main suspect, he would be happy. But he clearly still had his doubts. She wasn't sure why. All he would say was he had a feeling in his gut.

The man was as stubborn as all heck, but still, she had feelings toward him. Whether that was because he had saved her life, she wasn't sure. Laura felt safe around Stan, but she was the same around Cade and Tommy.

She couldn't explain it, but the way she felt about her fake husband was different. Oh, she'd heard about women who fell in love with the men who had saved them. That wasn't her. Laura was different to most women. She was strong and independent. She didn't rely on men to look after her, and she certainly didn't let them tell her what to do.

Laura made a vow there and then – she would not fall in love with Stan. Besides, he was not interested and had mentioned their annulment even before they were married. He reiterated it afterwards as well.

It proved how determined he was of severing their relationship, if you could call it that. Well, she could be just as decisive as Stan about an annulment. If she could do it now, Laura knew she would.

~*~

Waking up next to Stan seemed wrong. Terribly wrong. Especially when his arms were wrapped around her and they lay in the most intimate position together.

Laura needed to get out of bed. She was enjoying being held in Stan's arms far too much. Yes, he was her husband, but it was only a ruse. She had no right to have feelings for him, and this…intimacy…was only making it worse.

She gently removed his arms from around her middle and slid out of bed. Snatching up her clothes, Laura headed toward the bathroom where she would freshen up, dress, and fix her hair. Then, and only then, would she feel equipped to face the day.

Staring at herself in the mirror, Laura noticed the dark shadows under her eyes. They'd only appeared after her father's death. And her kidnapping.

She expected they would disappear now she was safely tucked away in Stan's home. But no, they were still there. It was the uncertainty of her future, Laura was certain.

Shaking her head, Laura knew she had to get such thoughts out of her mind. She had a job to do, and that was feed the men protecting her. Without a full belly, they couldn't function. Her governess drummed it into Laura for much of her young life.

Not that she'd ever intended getting married. It wasn't something she ever wanted to do. But now, here she was. Pretending to be Stan's wife and behaving as though she truly was.

Movement in the house startled her. With her heart pounding loudly, Laura moved slowly toward the kitchen. The sound seemed to come from that direction. With no weapon to defend herself, she almost backed off. Retreating to Stan's bedroom would be the best idea, she was certain.

Except she didn't want to wake him. Instead, she pushed forward. If it was her kidnapper, she would go quietly. That way her ordeal would be over, and Stan's life could go back the way it was before.

As she stood in the doorway, Laura's eyes were drawn to the silhouette of a man. He stared at her, his eyes glowing. Laura gasped. The silhouette stood, spun around, and Laura saw a gun. It was pointed toward her heart.

She suddenly felt light-headed and dropped to the floor.

Chapter Eighteen

Stan heard the thud and jumped out of bed. He didn't even stop to pull on his trousers. He did reach for his gun and headed toward the sound.

What he found was Tommy leaning over Laura. The scene before him seemed surreal. Tommy couldn't have shot her, or Stan would have heard it. "What happened?" he asked, trying to keep the emotion out of his voice.

"I think she fainted." Tommy was so matter of fact, but he was always like that. Just the facts and little more.

Stan glared at him. "What did you do?" His words sounded accusatory, even to Stan.

"I…I pointed my gun at her. I didn't realize it was Laura. I thought someone had broken in."

"Broken in? With you guarding the only door?" This is exactly the reason Stan wanted to be part of the team guarding her. Instead, he slept through it all.

"You're right," Tommy said. "I'm sorry. I half realized it was Laura or maybe you or Cade. But I had to be certain." He rubbed a hand through his hair before speaking again. "We both know it's true."

Stan shuddered. His former partner was correct. You could not second guess criminals. They were sneaky creatures. The day you let your guard down was the day a bullet ended your life.

He reached down and picked up his wife. She seemed far more frail laying in his arms like this. Her face was taunt and worried. Stan carried her into the bedroom and placed her gently on the bed. As he pulled the covers up around her, Laura began to stir.

She glanced up at him with those soulful blue eyes of hers. "What happened?" she whispered.

Stan sat on the side of the bed. He caressed her cheek, knowing he had no right to do so. "You fainted," he told her quietly. Anger rose in him over the circumstances, despite knowing what Tommy did was protocol. "Tommy pointed a gun at you. He was ensuring no one broke in."

"You're angry?" she asked, then studied him.

The silence of the room hit him hard. Laura continued to study him but said nothing more. Then he recalled her question. Stan reached for her hands.

"Of course I'm angry. With Tommy," he said. Would it be enough to cover up his absolute concern over her safety?

His heart pounded and she stared into his face. Laura didn't say a word for the longest time. Did she understand he was trying to keep her calm? "Don't be angry. There's no point. I'm grateful Tommy was doing his job. I didn't even think about the fact he might be in the kitchen." She shook her head then. "In reality, this is my fault. I should have told him I was there."

Except she must have thought he was her abductor. Either way, it may not have been a better outcome than what they already faced.

"It's not your fault," Stan said. "But I will admit it wasn't Tommy's fault either. Just a misunderstanding," he said as he shrugged his shoulders.

"I can tell you're still angry," she whispered. "But what about the man at the window?"

"Man at the window?" he sputtered.

Laura gazed at him. "I…I don't think I dreamed it," she told him. "I…"

Stan cut her off. "Tommy!" he shouted, not wanting to leave Laura alone. Not for even a moment.

The second Tommy was by his side, Stan relayed what Laura had said. His shock could not have been more profound. "Which window?" he asked, trying to his face blank. The urgency in his voice said otherwise.

"The main door window." Before she stopped speaking, Tommy was gone. Stan heard movement coming from the other end of the house. Cade. Definitely better than one man if someone had broken into the workshop. How he managed that, Stan didn't know. The doors and walls to the workshop were sturdy. They would be almost impossible to break through. Stan believed them to be impenetrable.

His heart pounded as he waited for a report from the two rangers.

Laura tried to sit up, but quickly laid down again. She didn't say the words out loud, but it was clear she was still light-headed. "Rest up. You don't need to do anything except take it easy." He lifted a hand to touch her cheek again, but stopped himself. Stan wasn't going to let himself fall for his wife.

Except he had to admit, but only to himself, it was already too late.

~*~

Tommy sat at the kitchen table opposite Stan, and it was clear he was upset. He opened his mouth to speak a few times but closed it again. Stan's first thought was to let him dwell in his guilt. Except he knew it wasn't the right thing to do. Especially to a man who had been his friend and partner for many years. "Laura is fine. You're fine, and no one was hurt."

The last part was the most important. It could easily have gone a different way. The fact was, Tommy was a professional. He had never discharged a firearm without good reason. Stan knew he wasn't about to start now.

"She could have been hurt. Killed even," Tommy said, his voice slightly above a whisper and full of regret. "Not necessarily by me, but whoever it was Laura saw."

"If she did see anyone," Stan said. "She was half asleep, and it was dark."

Studying him, Stan decided different tactics were required. "I don't think her abductor wants her dead. Not now, anyway. He wants to marry her and collect her inheritance. I'd hoped if I married Laura, he would crawl in whatever hole he crawled out of and leave her alone."

"Except we both know it doesn't work that way," Cade insisted. Of course he was right.

"Perhaps the message didn't get out about our marriage," Stan said. "Not if he is still trying to abduct her."

"We found no sign of a break-in, and there was no one in the workshop," Tommy said. "Do you think she imagined it?"

Stan shook his head, but knew Tommy was likely right. Laura was under stress. The kitchen was dark. Perhaps she'd seen Tommy's reflection in the window? He really didn't know, but he would alert the sheriff first thing in the morning.

The three men sitting around the table were a team and had been for many years. They worked together well.

Apart from the fact Laura was in danger, he'd enjoyed trying to work out the puzzle of her kidnapping. It was in his blood. He'd known it decades ago when he decided to join the Texas Rangers, and he knew it now.

Stan hated to admit it, but he was too old to go back into active duty. He felt old. The day he hit forty, his entire mindset changed. He was already in Harrietville, assisting his father, who was too frail to continue working. Jonathon Munro was beyond stubborn and refused to lay down his tools.

Whether it was a ruse to get Stan to stay, he wasn't sure. It had been almost two decades since Stan had done any stonemason work. With his father's help, he slipped back into the routine of many years ago.

His few months leave of absence became two years. Stan's life had completely changed, and he wasn't unhappy about it. Instead of chasing down murderers and robbers, he now fashioned blocks of stone into beautiful works of art.

He especially enjoyed creating decorative fireplaces. They would sit for decades as pride of place in homes around town. Gravestones were not his favorite thing to do, but it was part of his job and was important to the loved ones left behind.

Alongside his father, Stan had worked on the archways that led into Harrietville. It was far from the outback town he originally believed it to be and enjoyed living here. Alone, with no one else to bother him.

Until now.

Laura had become important in his life. Not because of her situation, it was more than that. He had felt it the first time he sat her in his cottage. There was far more to her than he initially expected.

Kidnap victim. Single woman. Heiress. Complicated story.

Added up, it meant far more than he ever expected it would.

Chapter Nineteen

Laura sat up slowly. She'd been on her way to cook breakfast when the…incident occurred. The silhouette of a man was visible due mainly to the light coming from the woodstove.

Limited light flowed through the windows too. She recalled the face at the window. Except that couldn't be true. Tommy would have seen it too, wouldn't he?

Her imagination was playing games with her.

If it wasn't so dangerous, Laura would leave right now. She was tired. Exhausted. It was the stress of the situation, she knew it was. Laura couldn't even imagine how the men were feeling. They put their lives on the line for her. Stan included.

It wasn't right. They didn't know her. None of them did. She knew Drake far better, and she wouldn't expect him to protect her either. He'd offered, several times, but she'd refused. Not once did Laura believe she was in any danger.

Never before had anyone tried to abduct her. Not while Father was alive.

Sitting on the side of the bed, Laura knew it was a completely different scenario now. With her father gone, she was the only stumbling block to the kidnapper's grab for her fortune. Forcing her into marriage would give him clear access.

A shiver went down her spine. What if he had succeeded? Would she have been eliminated when he was assured he had control of Hartley Textiles? Merely thinking about it was enough to have Laura feeling lightheaded again.

She gasped as a shadow came over her.

"It's only me," Stan said, then sat down beside her. "I came to check on you. Are you feeling any better?" He put an arm around her waist, and Laura felt comforted. She rolled herself into him, and Stan wrapped her in his embrace.

They stared into each other's eyes. They both knew they shouldn't be doing this, but it was clear neither wanted to move. Laura leaned her head against Stan's chest. She listened to his strong and steady heartbeat.

As much as she should protest, she had no intention of doing so. She glanced up into his face. Stan's face seemed softer, gentler, somehow. His fingers came up under her chin and he leaned in. It was clear he was going to kiss her.

Laura had no thought of stopping him.

"Tell me if you want me to stop," he whispered. His words were so quiet, she barely heard them.

"Don't stop," she said quietly. They may not intend to stay together, and likely wouldn't. Right now, she wanted to be comforted by the man she'd married.

Even if that marriage was only make believe, she felt a connection to Stan. A bond like none she'd felt before. Not with anyone.

He saw her for who she was, not how much money she had.

With her father gone, Drake would have insisted she have a prenuptial agreement drawn up, but Laura knew it wasn't necessary in this case.

Stan was not interested in her money. He was barely interested in her as a woman. Except now he was kissing her. Soft. Gently. His arms still holding her close. His hand came up and touched her cheek, and he pulled back from her lips.

His eyes drew her in. They were the most beautiful eyes she'd ever seen. Laura wondered what he'd seen with those eyes. What awful things he'd had to deal with over the years he'd been a Texas Ranger.

She would probably never know. And rightly so.

"Stan," she said gently. "We shouldn't. Not if we are going to annul our marriage." Laura knew she was right, but still didn't want Stan to stop.

"Is that what you want?" he asked. "For me to stop?" His eyes implored her, and Laura knew it was not what she wanted. With all her heart, she wanted Stan. She wanted to live here in his cottage where she felt at home. And she dearly wanted to spend the rest of her life with this man.

Except Laura knew she had no choice. She had to oversee her father's business. It was the agreement she'd made with him. A verbal agreement, but still a promise is a promise, and she couldn't go back.

"I must return to Helena after all this unpleasantness is over," she said.

Stan pulled back and stared into her face. "Unpleasantness? Is that what we are calling it?" He removed his hands and stared down at her. His eyes were filled with sadness, and Laura knew exactly how he was feeling. She felt it too.

If Laura had her way, she would never return to Helena. Or her father's business. Drake was more than capable of running the business himself. She could give him free reign and let him employ someone to help him.

It was a good plan, but would she ever get to carry it out? Would her abductor get his hands on her before Laura could put it all in place?

Laura stood. Her head was spinning, but she wouldn't tell Stan. He would fuss over her, she was certain.

"What are you doing?" he demanded, keeping his voice low.

She stared down at him. Did he think he could tell her what to do now they were married? "I'm doing what I set out to do earlier. Breakfast won't make itself," she said firmly, and hurried out of the room.

Both Cade and Tommy sat at the table cradling a mug of coffee. She heard Stan behind her but ignored his presence.

Tommy shook his head. It was only a slight movement, but Laura noticed. She sighed. They hadn't found any trace of the man at the window. Of that she was certain. Perhaps she had dreamed it after all.

The image stayed with her. Laura knew she'd seen the man before. But where? The more she thought about it, the more frustrating it became.

Without asking, she poured coffee for Stan, and made tea for herself. It may be presumptuous, but she sat down at the table with the three men. "I know him," Laura said. All three stared at her. "The man in the window. I know him."

She noticed the glances they had between each other. They might have been fleeting, but they were there. Laura ignored them.

"Do you have your suspect list?" she asked Stan, and he reached into his pocket for the list. Laura stared down at the words he'd written. Predictably, he had Drake at the top of his list.

Drake Simmons – Joseph Hartley's assistant

Undertaker

Undertaker's assistant

Gravediggers (transients)

Doctor (signed death certificate)

The longer she stared at the words before her, the more convinced Laura was there was someone missing. She tapped her fingers on the paper in front of her. She closed her eyes for clarity. Perhaps it would come to her without distractions.

She could feel the eyes of the three men bore into her. "Someone is missing," she said quietly, her eyes still closed. She was trying to conjure up the man in the window again, but her mind was not letting her.

Laura suddenly opened her eyes and pushed her chair back. "I don't have time for this," she said, knowing full well what she really meant was it was playing with her mind. If she didn't try so hard, it might come to her.

She reached for her apron. The one Stan had purchased at her request, then headed into the pantry to collect the ingredients for the men's breakfasts. Bacon and eggs with toast. How many times had she made that same breakfast for her father? Too many to count.

She'd even made it for her father's attorney.

Laura screamed. She didn't mean to, but it simply came out. The sound of running startled her, and moments later, the three men stared at her from the entrance of the pantry. "Harrison Lockwood," she said, her voice a little shaky.

All three stared at her curiously. "Harrison Lockwood," Stan repeated.

"Father's new attorney. Harrison had only recently taken over the business after his father retired." She thought for a moment. "Harrison complained about the retainer his father had agreed to. Said it wasn't enough." She grimaced. "Most of the time he did nothing but was paid anyway. It was a very generous retainer."

"Harrison didn't think so?" Stan asked.

The more she talked about Harrison Lockwood, the more ill Laura felt. "I always felt uncomfortable around him. Not his father, though," she quickly added. "Harrison believed their services were worth far more and after his retirement, tried to change the agreement his father made." She shook her head. "It was a legal contract, signed by his father and mine."

The three men exchanged glances again.

"Is that who you saw in the window, Laura," Cade asked gently.

"I believe it is," she said. "My father never underpaid anyone. Pelham Lockwood was paid a monthly stipend that was equivalent to almost a year's wages for most attorneys. Even if his services were not required."

"And yet, his son still wanted more. I believe we found our kidnapper," Stan said firmly. "All we have to do now is locate him."

Chapter Twenty

Apart from the fact someone, most likely Laura's abductor, infiltrated the building he believed completely impenetrable, Stan felt relieved. Finally, they had a genuine suspect. Not that he was ruling out Drake Simmons. At least not until he had confirmation from the sheriff.

What he did know was they needed to search his workshop again. This time more thoroughly.

The men stepped aside as Laura pushed her way out of the pantry. No matter what, she intended to make breakfast. Stan could see her determination. She wreaked of it.

He knew that no matter what happened, Laura would ensure the three of them were fed. Any other time, he might decide it was a good trait to have. Right now, though, he'd rather she let them go about their duties and search his workshop. Again.

Harrison Lockwood must be a devious creature. How else could Cade and Tommy search his workshop and not find the man? He couldn't think of anywhere a grown man could hide and not be found.

The biggest question was, how did he get in? Stan had ensured his workshop was secure, along with his home. Not for himself, but for his father. Jonathan Munro was frail. If anyone entered his home, who knew what they might do.

Stan had not intended to stay for long, but it was soon clear his father needed full time care. The only way to provide it was to go on a leave of absence from the Texas Rangers.

In his mind, Stan scanned his workshop. There were crates all around the perimeter. They each contained blocks of stone. There was no room for a child to crawl inside, let alone a grown man. He shook himself mentally.

Stan was thinking too hard. When he did that, answers did not present themselves, only more questions. Instead, he would take in the delicious aroma of breakfast cooking.

"Sit down," Laura demanded, then loaded each plate with food. As she placed a plate in front of each man, she studied them. One by one.

Stan couldn't help but wonder what she was thinking. The most likely scenario, he decided, was whether they would find this so-called attorney before he was able to snatch her away again.

She turned back to the stove and dished herself a much smaller meal. Instead of eating, she pushed her food around the plate. "Not hungry?" Stan asked. She frowned, then glanced up at him.

"Nervous, I guess," Laura told him. "And worried. What if Harrison is still here?" She glanced around the room then, her gaze falling on each window.

It got Stan to thinking. "Which window was he staring into?" he asked. Although she'd already told them, perhaps she'd gotten it wrong.

Laura lifted her mug of tea to her lips. "The one over the sink," she said as she glanced at it again. A shiver went through her, and Stan admonished himself for upsetting her again. On the other hand, he knew it was a question that had to be asked.

As it turned out, it needed to be asked.

With that short sentence, he knew exactly how Harrison Lockwood had managed to stare at Laura through the window.

~*~

With breakfast finished, Laura cleared away the breakfast dishes. She wiped down the table, and began to wash the plates, cutlery, and utensils used to make breakfast.

Stan sat at the kitchen table watching her every move. Cade and Tommy did exactly what Stan suggested and went out onto the street. The pair followed Stan's instructions and went to the street side of his house.

As he relayed to them, there was no entrance there, only at the front. But there was a tall fence. It was built to discourage anyone from trying to enter the property. The height of the fence was almost equal to the roof. At one time, there was a small vegetable garden. It was now nonexistent, along with the back entry to the home.

Believing it to be hazardous for his father, Stan had removed it and sealed the building from that side.

"This has all been a huge inconvenience," Laura told him as she hung up the apron. "To you especially, but also to Tommy and Cade. The sheriff, too."

She sighed, and Stan could hear her frustration. He also was frustrated. Getting information about Drake Simmons was proving difficult. He needed to confirm the man was at the office and was still there, before he would eliminate him. With Helena being so far away, he had no choice but to wait it out.

Laura studied him. "You still think it's Drake, don't you?" She didn't sound annoyed this time, only curious.

"What I think doesn't matter. We follow the evidence. This attorney, Harrison Lockwood – he sounds like a real charmer." He remembered the way Laura shivered when she spoke his name and talked about the man. "Sometimes gut instinct tells you more about a person than any rap sheet can." He scrubbed his hand across his chin. His face was bristly. "I need a shave," he said out loud, not meaning to.

Laura smiled. "Yes, you do." She stood then and strode into the sitting room. Stan followed her and poked at the fire. He filled it with fuel and got it burning to full capacity again. When he glanced over his shoulder at her, Laura was staring at him. Was she merely watching the fire, or was she watching him?

Stan shoved that last thought away. She might have allowed him to kiss her, but she wasn't truly interested in him. He knew all along she'd only stay until it was safe to go back home.

He heard the voices of the two rangers before they arrived in the sitting room. "Someone has definitely been there," Cade said. "There's a ladder tucked neatly against the fence. There was no one about, though."

"The sheriff expects to have an answer about the assistant soon," Tommy told them. "We ran into him doing his rounds. He'll come over as soon as he has news."

Laura stared at the pair. Was she concerned about what the sheriff learned? "Warm yourselves by the fire," she said quietly. "You must be cold."

Cade glanced at Stan. They both knew she wanted to say forget about Drake, it's not him. Stan was coming to the conclusion she was right but had to prove it before he believed it.

"Coffee anyone?" Laura said as she stood. It was clear to Stan, and likely everyone else that Laura did not like being idle. She rarely sat still for more than minutes. She was someone who needed to be busy.

Stan was once like that. He knew how she felt. Being a Texas Ranger meant when one assignment ended, another began. Often immediately, or within a day or two of the last one.

"Tell me about your charity work," Stan said, with one purpose only – to keep her in the sitting room. Watching her cook, clean, bake, then start the process all over again was exhausting. He could only imagine how Laura felt doing all that physical work.

She gazed at him. For a minute there, Stan was convinced she knew what he was doing. Trying to take her attention away from her dangerous situation. "I do whatever I can," she said quietly. "I don't usually talk about it. Those in need get my attention. I don't expect to receive accolades for doing what any decent person would do."

Laura gazed into his face. He felt like a little boy who had been admonished by his mother. "Now, if you are done, I'll make coffee," she said, then left him staring after her as she retreated to the other room.

Chapter Twenty-One

Laura knew exactly what Stan was doing. What did he stand to gain by keeping her in the sitting room?

As far as she could tell, absolutely nothing.

The constant chatter in the other room was not calming. In fact, it was the exact opposite. She'd relished being there, near to the fire, but with so many people in the room, it was no longer peaceful.

On the other hand, the kitchen was quiet. At least for now. If the men decided to sit at the table, then she would again retreat to the sitting room.

Laura pulled four mugs down from the cupboard and placed them on the countertop. She supported herself against the cupboard as she waited for the kettle to finish boiling. There was leftover cake from yesterday, and she would offer that to the men. Today would require more baking.

Not that she didn't like to bake – she enjoyed it. Closing her eyes, she savored the quiet of the small kitchen. The shuffling of feet interrupted her few moments of quiet. Arms surrounded her, and she knew it was Stan. She was becoming used to his presence, and his unique aroma.

Laura opened her eyes and glanced up at him. He smiled down at her. She was really going to miss those small moments they had together. Just the two of them.

She leaned into him. Nothing would spoil this time they had together. Alone. With no one else to interrupt them.

It was then she heard it. "Listen," she whispered. It wasn't as though she could be heard outside this room, or indeed the cottage.

Stan stiffened. His gentle arms became rigid. He leaned in and kissed her forehead, his eyes full of regret. "I need to sort this," he told her, then strode into the sitting room.

Her heart thudded. Would her nightmare soon be over? Or would her pursuer slip through their fingers yet again?

Moments later, the two rangers, guns in hands, ran through the kitchen and out into the workshop. Stan followed them, but Laura knew he would return shortly.

No point in making coffee for Tommy and Cade until they returned. Stan on the other hand could surely use an explosion of coffee to calm his nerves.

Laura knew tea would calm her, and she made a small pot of tea while she waited.

When he returned, Stan was not alone. Sheriff Colt Turner accompanied him. "Mrs. Munro," he said. It was then Laura knew something was up. Why was the sheriff being so formal?

"Coffee, Sheriff?" she asked, then poured one for him without waiting for an answer. She motioned for him to sit down, then placed the mug of hot coffee in front of him.

The sound Laura heard only minutes earlier was there again, only far louder this time.

"Rats in the roof, Stan?" Colt asked.

Stan tried not to grin. "More like a rat *on* the roof." He chuckled then. "Do you have news?"

A shiver went down Laura's spine. She was convinced Drake was innocent, and now the sheriff would confirm it. If he was not able to give her the news she expected… No! Drake would not harm her in any way. She'd known him for too long to believe he would do such a thing.

"Sheriff Boyle, from Montana sent a telegraph message." He reached into a pocket and pulled out the message. "I have interviewed several people, and the person of interest," He stopped reading to explain. "He means Drake Simmons." Then went back to the telegraph again. "The person of interest has attended the office every day. He has not been absent for even an hour, except when he reported Miss Hartley missing."

Tears filled Laura's eyes. It was exactly as she'd expected but was still a massive relief. "What did I tell you?" she asked, her voice full of emotion. There was no accusation in her tone, only validation of her beliefs.

She swiped at her eyes, then turned her back to the men. Laura poured her tea, then sat at the table, choosing a chair close to Stan. "I told you from the start it wasn't Drake. He has always been a loyal and diligent worker, and friend to my father."

"We had to confirm it for ourselves," Colt told her. "You understand, don't you?"

Laura nodded, then lifted the mug to her lips. She took a sip of the hot beverage before answering. "I do understand. I'm glad you were able to eliminate Drake from your enquiries."

A loud bang startled her. Laura stood, causing her chair to topple.

Stan reached for her. He didn't say a word. He didn't need to. Cade and Tommy were having trouble capturing the man who kidnapped her.

The sheriff stood. "I'll go and see if I can help," he said. Stan saw him out. Laura knew he would quickly return.

Her heart was pounding, and she felt weak. Laura sat at the table again, for fear she would collapse. Despite knowing Stan had secured the workshop and no one could enter without him unlocking the door, she worried about his safety. And that of the three lawmen.

"I'm back," Stan called before entering the kitchen.

The movement on the roof became even louder than before. "What are they doing up there?" she asked Stan.

"Arresting your kidnapper," Stan said matter-of-factly.

Laura had to believe he was right.

~*~

By all accounts, Laura's ordeal was over.

She corrected herself – it was almost over. The sheriff wanted her to identify the prisoner, since he refused to confirm his details.

Laura braced herself.

Stan stood by her side, his arm around her waist. With her husband, albeit a fake marriage, she could endure anything.

"You're shaking," Stan told her. "He is behind bars and cannot touch you. The sheriff only needs you to confirm he has Harrison Lockwood in his jail cell."

Laura nodded as they stood in the middle of the sheriff's office. Tommy and Cade stood nearby. They were a little worse for the encounter, with both bearing bruises and cuts. Harrison had not made it easy for them to arrest him.

"Ready?" Stan's reassuring voice calmed her.

She nodded again, then took a tentative step forward. Stan moved with her. He tightened his grip on her, and Laura rolled into him. Being held by this man lessened her apprehension for what she was about to do.

It was a cowardly thing to do, and Laura knew it. Instead of pushing her away, Stan held her close. "Ready?" hc asked again, then kissed her forehead.

Laura rolled her shoulders, then walked stiffly into the area where the prisoner was held.

"Laura," Harrison said, his voice almost begging. "Tell them they've made a mistake."

Wanting to laugh out loud at his ridiculous statement, but controlling her response, Laura turned to the sheriff. "This pathetic excuse for a man is Harrison Lockwood," she said, then spun around, ready to leave the room. Stan reached for her hand, squeezing it gently, then led her out of the room.

Her heart pounded uncontrollably. Finally, her ordeal was over.

Chapter Twenty-Two

Stan stared at his wife. All color had drained from her face, and she was ashen.

He knew it would be an ordeal for her, but he hadn't realized how difficult it would be. "Laura," he whispered. "Are you alright? It's over." He hoped his words would be comforting, but they didn't seem to help.

Lifting her in his arms, Stan placed her on one of the chairs in the sheriff's office. He worried she would faint, and knew it was still possible.

Sheriff Turner walked into the room. "I'm truly sorry you had to endure that," he said. "That man is a blight on society."

Laura said nothing for almost a minute. It was like she was in a trance, but Stan knew it was shock. Finally coming face-to-face with her abductor would not have been easy. Especially after everything he put her through.

"Maybe we should get the doc," Stan said quietly. His words meant for Cade.

Shocking them all, Laura stood. It was clear she was lightheaded, as her arms went out to steady herself. He clasped Laura around the waist. "I don't need the doctor," she said, ignoring the fact he was basically holding her up. "What I need is fresh air, then to go home and have a cup of tea."

Stan studied her. *Home? Did she mean his home? Their home?* It was, of course, one and the same. His heart soared at the possibility of Laura staying with him for the rest of their lives.

What if she changed her mind when the shock wore off? He didn't want to think about it.

Leading her outside, Stan kept a firm grip on his wife. She was unsteady, but she was determined to get there under her own steam. They sat on the wooden bench situated outside the sheriff's office.

She breathed in the fresh air, and Stan was surprised at seeing the color return to her face. Even her eyes seemed more focused.

"It was wrong, what he did," Laura said gruffly.

Stan wasn't sure what she was referring to. There was so much Harrison did that was wrong, that went against everything right.

"He shouldn't have attacked Tommy and Cade," she said firmly, despite the emotion in her voice.

Despite everything Harrison Lockwood did to her, Laura was concerned about the lawmen being injured as they tried to arrest him. "They have endured far worse," Stan told her. "Cuts and bruises are nothing. The doc will check them over, if that reassures you."

Laura sat straight on the uncomfortable wooden bench. "It would." She sighed as though a huge weight had been lifted from her shoulders. Laura then turned to face him. "Thank you."

Stan had done little to help. He'd been banned from the investigation, with good reason. He had more or less comforted Laura this entire time. And protected her with all his heart.

"Drake Simmons has been notified the kidnapper has been caught and arrested," Stan whispered. "He'll be here in the next day or two to take you home."

Stan had heard the expression, *if looks could kill*, but had never before experienced it. Not only did she glare at him, but Laura pursed her lips. It was clear she was angry, but he wasn't certain why. "Is there a problem?" he asked gently.

She stared straight ahead. "Do you hate me so much, you can't wait to rid yourself of me?" Her eyes filled with unshed tears. "What if I don't want to leave?"

Confusion filled Stan. "You don't want to leave? I thought you wanted an annulment."

Laura reached over and pulled him to her. "I don't want one. It was you who said you wanted an annulment. Do I even get a choice?" she asked, her voice barely above a whisper.

Stan's head was swimming. He held her close and whispered in Laura's ear. "I changed my mind days ago," he said. "When I fell in love with you. Did you honestly believe I would kiss you if I planned to dissolve our marriage?"

Laura laid her head against his chest. "I don't want to leave," she said firmly. "I love you, Stan. It seemed foolish to feel this way, since we are practically strangers, but it's out of my hands."

She glanced up at him, and Stan knew there was nothing else left to do. He leaned in and kissed the woman he loved.

~*~

Two days later Drake Simmons arrived. His initial confusion turned to happiness when he discovered Laura had no intention of leaving Harrietville. "I still cannot believe Harrison Lockwood did this to you," he said. "More than anything, I am still trying to process you married a total stranger." He studied Stan, who grinned.

"I am certainly the winner here," Stan said. "The circumstances weren't the best, but it has all turned out fine."

"No prenuptial," Drake mumbled, but his words were still audible.

"My life was in danger. Stan stepped in when I needed help. Besides, he's not interested in my money." Laura braced herself for the next conversation. "Can we talk business?" she asked Drake.

"Of course," he answered, his voice strained. Did he expect bad news?

"I am appointing you general manager of the business. You will have a free hand to run it however you see fit. Employ additional staff to assist you – I don't want you overworked."

Drake's eyes lit up. Did he not see this coming? "Thank you, Laura. I won't let you down."

"I am certain of it," she told him. "There are other important things to sort out, but we need to find a solicitor to make it all official. Before I forget – Father wanted me to gift you a lump sum. He didn't put it in the will as, according to Harrison Lockwood, it was too messy. We now know otherwise."

Drake was silent as he took it all in. "It's not necessary," he finally said. "I am paid handsomely for my work."

"No argument," Laura said firmly. "I will ensure an amount fitting of your skills, expertise, and loyalty is deposited in your account forthwith." Her words were firm and left no room for discussion.

"I've brought some of your clothes," Drake said, completely changing the subject. Laura gathered he'd done it on purpose, but didn't push the issue. There would be time later to discuss the business further. For now, she was grateful to have some of her belongings.

She stepped forward and hugged Drake. There was never any doubt in Laura's mind that Drake was involved in her kidnapping.

Epilogue

Two years later…

Stan stood patiently next to Bobby Carlson, watching his apprentice's every move. "A little more to the left," Stan told him. Stan remembered the days when he was the apprentice, and his father was teaching him.

Jonathon Munro was far more patient than Stan would ever be. Back then, Stan wasn't particularly interested in learning the trade passed down through generations. He wanted to be a Texas Ranger – it was as simple as that. Bobby was the complete opposite.

His apprentice glanced up at him. "Like this?" he asked.

The almost twenty-one-year-old was better than Stan ever was. "Perfect," Stan told him. "You are doing so well." The young man's eyes lit up. It would be years before Bobby would perfect his trade, but once he did, he would open up a whole new career, and an entirely new life for himself. It would come with experience.

It felt good to help the community in this way. Before Laura came into his life, Stan kept to himself. Now, with his wife by his side, Stan had insinuated himself into the community. He joined in many of the neighborhood functions, goaded by Laura.

"Mail for you, Stan," the postmaster told him, then handed over an envelope. "Well, you and Laura." He disappeared as quickly as he arrived.

Stan glanced at the sender's details. Drake Simmons. He already knew what this would be. A photograph. Laura's pet project. She was still doing charity work, but now she did it without leaving home. "Keep going," he told Bobby. "I won't be long."

He stepped inside the cottage and handed the large envelope to Laura. "You open it," Stan told her. "I know how special this is to you."

The joy on her face filled him with warmth. Laura tore open the envelope and removed the photographs inside. When she made the decision to relocate to Harrietville, to remain Stan's wife, Laura also decided to continue her charity work. Except this project was too big for not only her, but Drake as well.

As a result, the Hartley Foundation was created. Drake had set up the foundation and employed staff to run it. Laura had insisted her former home, which she described as an oversized palace, should be turned into an orphanage. A trust was set up to ensure there was always money to fund the orphanage for years to come. Part of the profits from the textile business would forevermore flow into the foundation.

The photographs she held in her hands confirmed the transition from mansion to functioning orphanage was complete. After showing Stan the photographs, she held them close to her chest. This was the project of her heart, so it made perfect sense.

"Drake says the foundation is now finalized, staff have been employed, and we can take in children as needed," she said. Laura didn't try to hide the emotion in her voice, and Stan pulled her close. As close as he could get anyway.

Her swollen belly made it rather difficult at times, but he still managed to hold her and show Laura how much he loved her. The sound of their six-month-old baby playing in his crib sent warmth through Stan.

Was it really only two years since Laura arrived in his workshop, looking for a safe place to hide? So much had happened in that time.

As he continued to hold his wife close, he felt a distinctive kick against his own belly. Stan grinned. "The little one is getting hungry," he said jokingly.

"No doubt, just like her daddy." Laura's words had him wondering. Would it be a girl this time, or another boy? A little girl would have him wrapped around her little finger, Stan was certain. Either way, provided the baby was healthy, that's all he cared about.

"Lunch is ready," Laura said, interrupting his thoughts about becoming a father again. "Go tell Bobby. Don't you have something to tell him today?"

He certainly did. It would be life-changing for the young man who was diligent in his work. He had a strong sense of ethics, and made Stan proud to be teaching him the trade Stan's own father so adored.

The moment the men sat down at the table, Laura placed bowls of soup in front of them both. She added still warm bread to a platter and sat it in the middle of the table, along with a stick of butter.

As Laura sat down, she motioned to Stan. No words were needed, he knew what she was trying to say. *The time has come.*

"Eat up," Laura said, when Stan didn't speak.

He was nervous, and knew Laura could tell. Trouble was, it had to be said. It wasn't like he didn't want to tell Bobby. He was simply nervous about it. "Bobby," he said carefully. "There's something we need to talk about."

Bobby shifted in his seat. He put down his spoon and glanced at Laura. "It's not terrible," she told him gently. "In fact, it's the opposite."

He brightened up a little, but still seemed cautious.

"Bobby," Stan said again. "I believe your twenty-first birthday is approaching?"

"Yes, Sir, it is. Next month."

Stan rolled his eyes. "What did I say about this *Sir* business?"

Bobby seemed more anxious than ever now. "Sorry, Stan."

Stan smiled. "Much better. Now, as I was saying, with your birthday coming up, Laura and I have a gift for you."

Bobby glanced from one to the other. "You have done so much for me. I don't need a gift."

"You'll want this one," Laura said, joy in her voice. "Go on, Stan, tell him."

It was clear Laura was enjoying watching him squirm. "How are you enjoying your apprenticeship?" Stan asked. "It's almost complete."

Bobby grinned. "I love it," he said. "I will hate when it all ends." Now he looked sad.

"Oh, for goodness sake, Stan. Either you tell him, or I will." Laura was becoming impatient with him.

Stan motioned for her to tell the young man who had shared their lives for the past two years.

"The crux of the matter is, Bobby, your gift is one that will change your life." Laura glanced at Stan who could see the young man was suddenly intrigued.

"Change my life?" He chuckled, and it was clear he didn't yet understand.

"This building, the cottage, the workshop, the business. Stan is signing it over to you. For your twenty-first birthday."

Bobby sputtered. "I…you…" The words wouldn't come.

"You are incredibly talented as a stonemason," Stan told him. "My little family are moving into a small ranch not far from Harrietville. It's where I want my children to grow up."

"But…I can't accept it," Bobby said, still clearly in shock.

"Too late to go back. All the paperwork is done, but you must wait for your birthday to make it legal."

Bobby was clearly dumb struck. Words didn't come, but Stan knew this would set Bobby up for the rest of his life.

Stan was filled with joy. It truly would be life-changing for Bobby. He'd worked hard learning the trade and deserved it. He knew without Laura's inheritance it wouldn't be possible. Stan was grateful for everything she had brought to him through her family's business, and yet, she never acted in a way that spoke of her wealth.

Thinking back to two years ago, Stan would never have dreamed any of this was possible. He had never believed in fate. Until Laura came into his life.

Satisfied with the arrangements they'd made for Bobby, he lifted his spoon and ate his soup. Then Stan reached for a slice of the warm bread Laura had made.

It was then he decided all was right with the world.

From the Author

Thank you so much for reading my book – I hope you enjoyed it.

I would greatly appreciate you leaving a review where you purchased, even if it is only a one-liner. It helps to have my books more visible!

About the Author

Multi-published, award-winning and bestselling author Cheryl Wright, former secretary, debt collector, account manager, writing coach, and shopping tour hostess, loves reading.

She writes historical romantic suspense and historical western romance.

She lives in Melbourne, Australia, and is married with two adult children and has six grandchildren, and three great-grandchildren.

When she's not writing, she can be found in her craft room making greeting cards.

Links

Website: http://www.cheryl-wright.com/

Facebook Reader Group:
https://www.facebook.com/groups/cherylwrightaut
hor/

Join My Newsletter:

https://cheryl-wright.com/newsletter/
(and receive a free book)

www.ingramcontent.com/pod-product-compliance
Lightning Source LLC
Chambersburg PA
CBHW071016180726
48291CB00004B/1481